THE FABRIC OF OBLIVION

JESSE LEE GUNN

Hollow Spire Press

The Fabric of Oblivion
Copyright © 2026 Jesse Lee Gunn

Published by Hollow Spire Press
Hayward, California

Cover art by Eryel Maurin

For information about permissions, please contact the publisher at jessegunn03@gmail.com

ISBN (Paperback): 979-8-9994171-0-7
ISBN (Ebook): 979-8-9994171-1-4
Library of Congress Control Number: 2025915902

First Edition: January 2026

For those who remain,
when the world asks them to vanish.

LETHE FLOWED, CEASELESS IN her apathy, the current quietly carrying threads away. On the shore, Penelope wove a tapestry even as it unraveled into the waters before her.

"Each night," she whispered, "I undo what the world believes is set and my story continues as long as I weave."

"Yet," Lethe murmured softly, "all threads eventually slip away."

Beside her, Ananke stood solemnly. "Every thread," Ananke intoned, her voice like a blade held against silk, "must follow the path already woven."

Penelope's grip tightened, continuing to weave, even as the river and fate patiently waited for each thread to fall.

Part One

Chapter 1

THE COFFEE WASN'T HOW she liked it. Too sweet, too much cream. Someone must have made a mistake at the counter.

She forced a sip anyway. She always did. There was no point in fixing it now, no reason to go back, no sense in making it a problem. It was easier to drink it as it was.

By the time she reached the subway station, she had already adjusted to the taste. She took another sip. She had forgotten to take her medication again. It wasn't intentional. It never was. But the mornings blurred together, and sometimes she just missed it.

Maybe that was why her limbs were heavier. Maybe not. She didn't know anymore. She was swept onto the train without thinking, drifting with the crowd, her feet falling into the rhythm of routine. She barely glanced up from her phone as the doors shut behind her.

She looked up at the map. The tracks looked like a fault-line running through her world. She squinted, allowing her eyes to blur. Suddenly, there were threads connecting the various train stops, the weaving of a tapestry of geometric shapes upon a loom. Each stop became a sanctum, mirrored into infinity.

Paths curved toward them in perfect loops. Nothing remained, unless it was aligned. But she had. The faultline quivered at the outer edge of the Loom. A scar held open by memory that refused to let go. Within that space, a wound. And her.

She blinked. Three stops passed. The doors slid open on a station she didn't recognize. Blue and white tile. Cracked ceramic in an unfamiliar pattern. This wasn't her train. Her stomach tightened. The route would get her close enough to work, only not the way she usually went. She had followed the wrong pattern. Stepped onto the wrong platform without even noticing.

It was fine, a minor mistake, a small detour. But as she watched the stations pass, something unsettling rooted inside her. She was just a body, floating without a name. She dissolved and reformed with each breath; and her coat, unraveling at the edges, scattered like wisps that mended and frayed again. Her fingers found a loose thread at the hem of her sleeve. She would get where she needed to go. She always did.

Was this tiredness? Not exactly. Tiredness was an ache that required effort; she was just not here. Her body moved, her hands functioned, but it was mechanical. Usually, she could close her eyes and drift through the routine perfectly. It gave her time to think. Time to imagine. Time to process what it meant to be within the world, but not welcomed by it.

The train stopped. She stepped onto the platform, and began walking. Her reflection stared back at her in the darkened glass of the train before it started up again. The station lights flickered behind her, catching in the round frames of her glasses, glinting off the thin metal. Her dark, layered hair fell an inch past her shoulders. In the harsh station lighting, each strand of her hair drifted. Of course, that wasn't true. She searched for the right words, narrating it all in her head. Her hair was *practical, accepted*. Keeping it from becoming wild was enough. Her face was sharp in places, softer in others, features suspended somewhere between hesitation and blankness.

There she was, same round glasses perched on her nose. Same face, same name. But the reflection was wrong in a way she couldn't place. For a heartbeat, a small hand was tucked into hers. She instinctively closed her fingers around it, but found only her own. Then the train shifted, and it was gone. Just a child on the platform behind her. She turned to look, but thought better of it and averted her eyes. A ripple juddered through her, as if her balance had pitched a half step off-center; it left her slightly misaligned in her own skin.

A woman nearby, a mother perhaps, glanced up and gave her a small, warm smile. *You look tired*, it seemed to say. It was still safe; better than looking strange.

A speaker crackled overhead, and she searched for the words again. *Harsh. Guttural.* "Medical emergency reported on the southbound platform. Please remain behind the yellow line. Emergency services are en route."

A siren blared, too close, too loud, ricocheting off tile and metal. The lights above her flickered once, then steadied.

Her body flinched and her breath caught high in her throat, refusing to settle; she moved without planning, stepping back until her shoulder met a support beam. The concrete pressed cool against her coat. Her fingers grazed the wall. It was gritty, unpolished, still vibrating faintly from the alarm. Across the track, people murmured, shifted. No one looked at her.

Oblivion leaned in, precise and indifferent. A pressure that commanded her to vanish.

The siren cut off and the unraveling stalled. In its failure, she remained, though perhaps not quite whole. The PA repeated itself, voice too calm to be kind. Then nothing. Just the soft exhale of the train pulling away. Nobody seemed bothered.

She moved on, leaving the station and walking toward the office. But the moment lingered. An idea that flashed like an anchor between worlds.

The office reeked of paper dust and printer ink, the kind of tang that seeped into fabric. The rhythm of keyboards clicking and phones ringing fostered a familiar background noise. One she had been scoured into.

She sat at her desk, posture straight, fingers moving over the keyboard, adjusting her glasses with controlled, precise movements. The neutral tones of her sweater and coat blended seamlessly into the office surroundings. She moved with practiced precision, the kind formed by years of momentum more than ease.

Katherine. Her lips nearly mouthed the word. That was the name printed on her ID badge. That was the name attached to every email she sent, every document she signed.

A notification appeared on her screen. Another task, another expectation. She clicked the email open, scanning the words without truly processing them. 9:47 AM. The time flickered in the corner of her monitor. She had adjusted to the drag of the morning. Or so it seemed. The certainty hadn't stuck and she was left grasping for something she couldn't explain.

"Katherine," came Dr. Harlan's voice from across the room; flat, clipped, efficient. She strained to identify the right word for his tone. "I need the patient data from last quarter compiled by noon."

"Of course." The response left her lips before she could think it through, well practiced and automatic. The way it always had been; the way it always would be. But the name settled on her shoulders, pressing down in a way she couldn't quite define. She felt it in the tightness of her collar. The way the fabric of her sweater scraped against her spine.

She took out a pen and began to doodle. Three oracles, gathering in a long-standing accord. Their robes trailing glyphs like memory. Faces smooth. She'd drawn them before. Off and on. Characters in a world that was entirely her own. A world that sometimes made more sense than the one she was in.

She drew the first oracle like a ripple spread across the veil. Less solid, more wavering. The second oracle was harsher. She pressed the pen down firmer with each line. Symmetrical with the first, but in a way that was dangerous. As if she had drawn the lines with a knife rather than her ballpoint.

But the third... The third was special. She drew them slightly off-kilter, reluctant to move in symmetry with the others. Off-center. Close enough. Their lines were less a declaration. More a murmur. She had drawn them from wonder rather than by design.

She finished the sketch, clicked her pen shut, and sighed. She had never disliked the name Katherine before. Not really. It had been given to her the way everything else had, without noise, without question.

Katherine was the name teachers read aloud without ever looking up. The name used when the school nurse called home. When her mother introduced her to strangers with a practiced smile. It had always been someone else's version of her; tidy, formal, default. She had never chosen it. Only worn it, like a uniform that kept her safely legible to others.

It was a clean inheritance. An expectation she had accepted without resistance, but never claimed as her own. It was the name of someone capable, reliable, agreeable. A name that fit neatly into forms and emails, that smoothed over introductions and kept things simple. It had been easy to wear, but it clung to her skin like fabric that had shrunk in the wash. Too tight, too restrictive. She had never fought it, but that didn't mean it had ever been hers. She kept typing.

By noon, the break room smelled like mediocre lunches. Conversations wove through the space, background noise that barely registered. She presided over the coffee machine, tracking the liquid swirl in her cup. She stirred with the kind of care that made it feel like precision mattered. As if timing the swirl might reveal prophecy.

The reflection from the fluorescents overhead cast the surface of the liquid in a muted glow.

It swirled. Polished obsidian inlaid with porcelain. Who was this figure, advancing through the dark liquid of her coffee? Nobody answered, of course. The unanswered. That felt right. Not a name, a title. He advanced through the... the hollow spire, she decided. His jacket trailed behind him like a sentence left unfinished. Only the scar on his jaw stood out. Sharp, deliberate. A deviation in an otherwise meticulous form.

He wouldn't have questioned the call. In the Loom, commands didn't need explanation. They initiated, and he responded. Particularly commands issued by the Edict. A godlike structure of mechanical gears and light, endlessly clicking into place.

The command echoed: "Erase the anomaly. Seal the fracture." The decree passed down through the oracles, reaching him like a ripple under glass. A triad of voices joined as one.

"Katherine?"

Priya's voice shattered the spire, twisting it into dark liquid in her cup. She was watching her with an easy smile. "You okay? You're zoning out."

She nodded, barely. Like she wasn't sure if she meant it. "Yeah. Just tired."

"Gotta grab some energy to go. Sara hates when I skip lunch, says that I'm grumpy when I come home," Priya muttered, biting into a protein bar anyway. "But who has time to eat when management's always looking for a reason."

She blinked, caught off guard. She didn't know what reason Priya meant. Or maybe she did, and didn't want to name it. Instead, she smiled and nodded. That was safer, for both of them.

Priya moved on, but she remained. Her pulse had quickened. Had she been zoning out? How long? Had anyone else noticed? Her fingers curled around the edge of her ID badge, pressing against the plastic. The name printed there was impersonal, almost foreign. She'd had another name once, one that had fit better, one that had felt like her. *Sable.* But no one had called her that in years. What if she didn't wear the ID badge? Would it matter? Would anyone say anything?

No. They would still call her Katherine. She went back to her desk.

The decision kept her inert. It shouldn't be this difficult. Her pen hovered over the designation log. *Katherine Mercier.* That was what she was supposed to write, what she always wrote. But today, for the first time, she hesitated. The unanswered would have complied. An order is an order. A decree is a decree. He's walked this corridor before. Other anomalies, other names. And yet... something was different. An image breached protocol. A glint of dark hair. A thought that wouldn't vanish. Fingers brushed the edges of his own. He advanced. Seamless movements against ceramic. Tap. Tap. Tap. His purpose was clear. She was not.

She stopped flicking the pen and bit the end of it instead. She could just write it. Finish the task. Keep moving. That would be easier. Her hand was too heavy, as if the act of writing was more effort than she could summon. She blinked hard, trying to focus, but her limbs ached with something deeper than exhaustion. *Write it. Move forward. Keep going.* She tightened her grip on the pen, and she imagined every eye in the room glancing at her. As if they knew she was about to trespass.

She recalled that one year she had sat next to Penelope in English class. The teacher had snapped at Penelope for mispronouncing a line from the play, loud enough for the whole room to hear, sharp enough to sting. Sable remembered lowering her head, trying to disappear behind her copy of the script. When the teacher called her next, "Katherine," she froze. She read the words perfectly, reliably. Being correct brought less attention. But then the teacher tapped her page, the empty name field at the top was an indictment.

She had moved on, but Sable's hand had hovered above the margin where she was supposed to write it.

Penelope had nudged her notebook closer without looking up. "You always freeze up at the easiest parts," she murmured, voice low enough not to carry. "Name's the only thing they can't mark wrong."

Sable had laughed, the kind of laugh that doesn't try to be heard but escapes without noticing. Then she wrote it. Only her middle name. *Sable.*

She blinked, and Penelope's whisper faded. A coworker laughed about something that probably didn't matter. Her hands grasped the form in her lap, fingers lightly brushing against the fabric of her coat. Her posture remained deliberately straight. The hesitation didn't pass. She left the form on her desk, blank.

Chapter 2

AN EMAIL NOTIFICATION FLAGGED on her screen. A standard request, nothing out of the ordinary. She hit reply and started to type a response. Only, her signature was already filled in at the bottom of the email. It stared at her. *Katherine Mercier.*

She stared back, her fingers brushing absently against the worn edge of her coat sleeve. She had written her name thousands of times before. She had signed forms, sent emails, introduced herself in meetings, always with the same certainty. *Katherine Mercier.* But now the letters were an alien artifact on her screen. Too sharp, too final. Her hands paused above the keys. The cursor pulsed, waiting.

She'd known people who changed their names because their bones demanded it. This wasn't the same, yet the quiet relief felt like its kin.

Maybe no one would notice if she changed it. Maybe they'd notice too much. The thought was absurd. She shook her head; not a decision to take lightly.

Of course, there were places the Edict had yet to claim. The faultline was one. It contained what the Loom refused. What the Loom could not reconcile. Here, the symmetry held only as long as it chose. She imagined the unanswered stepping through it, sword still sheathed.

And there she was. The anomaly. Only, the word was imprecise. The command to erase was simply too clean. Like an axe swinging at a ghost already gone. He shouldn't look, but he couldn't take his eyes off of her.

And she just... stared back. She didn't flinch, even as he approached. Almost like she was waiting for him. He began to reach for his sword. Only, the decree faltered. Stuttered. Fell. He tasted smoke, and strangely... coffee that was too sweet.

She pushed the sketch aside, then flipped her notebook over, burying it. Then she clicked send, sealing the name in place. The knot in her stomach refused to loosen.

A pallid sheen flattened every surface of the conference room. Residual disinfectant marked the table, sharp in a way that clung to the back of the throat; it got under her nails, threaded through the fabric of her coat. A low hum droned from the projector in the corner, gears grinding their way through a slide deck of performance metrics no one really cared about.

Sable sat near the middle of the table, swallowed by the room. Her hands were folded neatly in front of her, posture carefully controlled, the lines of her blouse unwrinkled. She reached up, brushing a stray strand of hair behind her ear, a movement so familiar she barely noticed doing it. She initiated the performance. The eye contact that was just enough. The head nods that indicated that she was listening. The discussion was routine, voices blending together in a monotonous stream of updates and deadlines. She wanted to scratch a doodle into the table. She balled her hands into fists on her lap and smiled larger instead.

"Before we get too far," Dr. Harlan, the Principal Investigator said, glancing up from his notes, "let's take a quick moment to introduce ourselves for the new team members. Just your name and role. Let's start over here."

And then it began. A name, a department, a practiced incantation. Polished, effortless, mechanical. The pattern woven, moving steadily around the room, a rhythm she had heard before, participated in before.

Five people away. Four. Three. The tightening in her chest began. It's just nerves. It doesn't mean anything. It had never been anything. Nobody noticed her eyes watering. Probably.

Two. One. And then a pause. A break in the rhythm.

Her mouth opened. Because it should. Because it always did. What if she didn't say it? The thought formed before she could stop it.

Dr. Harlan prompted her. "Katherine?"

The name sat waiting. It would take nothing to say it. A repositioning of the tongue. Less effort than turning a page. But the room was already moving. The stage had already been set. And a break in this, even in the smallest way, was like a break in the world's own geometry.

For a moment, the cold steel of the Edict's judgement was visible in everyone's eyes, watching her. Waiting for her to choose.

It wasn't that she had chosen to be Katherine. It was simply easier not to fight. She started to form the words. She took too long. The weight of every other moment pressed down; every introduction she had given, every signature, every unchecked instance where the name had been spoken for her.

"Katherine Mercier, Clinical Data Specialist. Sorry, I wasn't ready to be perceived." The words were out.

The wheel kept its revolution. Grinding. The next person spoke. The introduction tasted like a lie. No relief arrived. Her mind drifted elsewhere.

Somewhere, a gear ground to a halt. A protocol failed. In the Loom, the unanswered flinched. Not from her, but for her. And for a moment, it was his skin that was unraveling.

He took an involuntary step back, shaken by a memory that wasn't his. Two figures, side by side in a room cast in golden light, and a choice denied. An observatory, perhaps. Slanted shadows and a warmth that didn't need to be explained.

She dropped the pen. Let it clatter louder than it should. Nobody seemed to notice. The meeting moved on without her. Voices blurred. Slides clicked forward. She rose too quickly, chair scraping the floor, murmuring something about needing air. No one looked up.

In the hallway, everything was too bright. The walls of the cage closed in. The building had been a government data center in the seventies. A concrete, brutalist shell that the company had cheaply retrofitted. They ran their modern algorithms on failing, sixty-year-old hardware, and it showed, painfully. Water stains bloomed on the faded acoustic tiles overhead like faded, forgotten maps. Everything smelled like old paper and sour wet concrete. The ballast hum wasn't just in the lights. It vibrated through the walls itself. A structural groan that threatened to colonize her bones. Every surface reflected a version of her she didn't recognize, glassed-over, deliberate, efficient.

She turned into the restroom on autopilot and stepped into the farthest stall. She sat down on the closed lid, jacket still buttoned, and pressed her fingertips to her temples. Her breath came shallow. The walls were thin, tiled, institutional. Fluorescent buzz hummed above her head. From a few stalls over, someone flushed and left without washing their hands. The door sighed shut. Silence returned.

Her hands shook. She tucked them between her knees, hating how familiar this kind of privacy felt. This ritual of breaking in places no one looked. And how she still felt like she was being judged for it.

A sticky note was taped to the back of the stall door. *Wash your hands, folks!* It was written in neat, looping script with a too-cheerful smiley face. She stared at it too long. Absurd. Friendly. Real. More real than the name she had just spoken into the room.

Katherine. It sounded like an apology. Like she was reaffirming someone else's expectation. She pulled a tissue from her pocket, folded it twice, and pressed it flat against her palm. Not to cry. Just to hold it.

What would the anomaly have said? Back in the meeting. "You hesitated. Why?"

After a few minutes, her breathing returned to something closer to normal. She stood, flushed nothing, washed her hands out of rhythm.

She sat again in the meeting, folding back into her chair as if nothing had happened. Her fingers curled slightly in her lap. The morning's reflection surfaced. How her hand gripped for one smaller. Not there.

Maybe she really was just tired. She couldn't tell anymore. Or maybe this was how it always was, and she had long stopped noticing.

Later, the office hummed with a calibrated calm, lights ticking above as screens blinked awake again. Sable stared at her inbox, barely aware of the emails piling up.

Priya's voice cut through the haze. "Hey, do you remember that summer that they rewrote the protocol, mid-study? When we were stuck doing overtime every weekend?"

Sable blinked, looking up. She straightened slightly, pushing her glasses up the bridge of her nose. Priya stood beside her desk, arms crossed, an amused glint in her eyes. "The one where we swore we'd quit but never did?"

But Sable was somewhere else. A version of herself, less careful, less arranged. A late night, laughter muffled behind stacks of homework.

Penelope's voice. "Sable, can we just get out of here already?" No hesitation. No second-guessing. A name spoken as if it belonged to her.

They had been mistaken for a couple often. By teachers, by cashiers, once by a nurse when Penelope showed up bleeding from the elbow. The nurse had asked Sable if her friend needed a translator. Penelope had raised an eyebrow and said, in perfect English, "Only when I'm unconscious." Sable had laughed, but Penelope hadn't.

"You know everyone thinks we're secretly in love," Penelope had teased one night, sprawled on Sable's bedroom floor with a half-eaten bag of popcorn between them.

Sable had shrugged. "They think everyone's in love. They can't imagine two girls like us just... being."

"Two girls like us?" Penelope teased, arching an eyebrow.

"I mean..." Sable had started, but Penelope had already moved on.

"Speak for yourself. I'm extremely lovable."

"You'd make a terrible girlfriend."

"But a great alibi."

They never talked about it again. There was nothing to clarify. She didn't know when Penelope's absence had started to feel like a wrong answer left on a test. Or when the name she gave the world started to feel like one. The memory stayed, stubborn and tender, refusing to dissolve. The unanswered wouldn't understand a memory like this. It wasn't his to hold. The thought clung to her for a second longer than it should have. She smiled to herself, then looked up to see if Priya had noticed.

Her fingers curled slightly against her desk. "Yeah. I remember."

Priya grinned back at her. "Brutal, right?"

Then her smile flickered, almost imperceptibly. "You zoned out again."

Sable blinked. "Oh, just a memory."

"Good or bad?"

"Both," she murmured, the words landing more as an admission than an answer. The faultline flexed beneath her; it listened. Her hand lowered to her side, something slipping loose.

Priya's eyes held her briefly, just enough to leave the door cracked.

"Anyway," Priya said, backing off. "I'm getting the hell out of here before they give me something else to do. See you tomorrow."

She moved on, but Sable watched the empty space where she had stood. She could have said something.

Could have asked something. Could have claimed some-thing. It passed. And she let it.

The Edict had named her anomaly. But even as she mouthed the word silently, it tasted false in her mouth.

Chapter 3

Cold seeped up from the wet pavement as she walked. The map of her world lived in her head, but the streets she walked on were unfamiliar beneath the sheen of rain. A chill, deeper than the cold of it, traced a line down her spine. Her hands instinctively pressed flat against her sides. She glanced down to confirm the flaps of her pockets were closed, buttoned. A small, practiced ritual of invisibility. She was safe. She would be safe. She was good at being unseen. She kept moving.

She glanced toward the darkened window of a closed bookstore as she passed. Near it, out of the rain, a black cat huddled under the awning, tail wrapped neatly around its paws. It wasn't grooming or looking for food. It just watched the street with a quiet, unnerving stillness. Its yellow eyes met hers. A look that was probably indifference, but could have been more.

It was the same cat she'd seen a dozen times before. A constant guardian carved from shadow in the corners of her world. An alleyway here, a fire escape there. A silent observer. A sentinel who watched, without alarm.

He existed beyond the faultline. A place that was wild, and overgrown. Vast and unmapped. Trees rose from the mist-cloaked floor like statues held in static. Their trunks were carved with names that no longer held meaning.

This cat, Sentinel, was perhaps a panther. The Loom might see her as an anomaly, a ghost stumbling through its ordered paths. But Sentinel saw a thread that hadn't yet been unspooled; he recognized her.

Her breath fogged in front of her. For a long moment, they just held each other's gaze. Then, slowly, she gave a single, small nod of acknowledgment.

The cat blinked once, a languid, unhurried response. Then it turned its head and began to meticulously clean a patch of fur on its shoulder. The message was clear: *I am watching. You may proceed.*

Sable moved on, the rain-slicked pavement feeling a little more solid under her feet. Pockets still sealed shut.

Her head ached. The day had unraveled her in ways she hadn't expected, but maybe it had been waiting to happen for a long time. Maybe she had been holding it together, piece by piece, until there was nothing left to grip.

August would see her and say her name like it belonged to her, and she would have to decide if she'd let him.

Sentinel wouldn't have led her here. That's not his role, and the cost of doing so was never paid. She imagined that they would have walked together, though. They'd pass remnants of the forgotten. A child's mask, worn smooth. A broken watch, its battery removed. A maple tree grown from the cracked pavement. Perhaps it teetered a little closer as she walked under its limbs.

The café pressed in. A clearing among the woods. A sacred place among the glades. Steam, coffee, perfume, voices. Outside, a tide of bodies passed, moving like they had somewhere else to be, as if they might someday arrive. As if they'd recognize it when it came. Inside, the quiet was curated. A hush had been arranged between every table like glass walls that rattled when anyone passed too close.

She sat across from August, their usual table tucked into the corner. A place where no one expected them to be anything other than themselves. A tension coiled inside her, unspoken and tight. She sketched absently. Letting the shadows pool around Sentinel's paws.

August studied her over the rim of his mug, his gaze unreadable. "Black coffee today? That's a change." He traced his cup with one fingertip, slow and looping; each motion looked deliberate, as if pacing something.

Sable's fingers tightened around the pencil, then let go. She gripped her mug instead. The contrast was stark against the cool air conditioning inside the café. "Just... not in the mood for sweet."

It wasn't entirely a lie. She wasn't sure anymore when it had started feeling this way, when the exhaustion had settled into her bones like it had always been there. She took a sip. It was bitter, and necessary.

August nodded along, gaze tracking the warmth curling up from his mug like it might rearrange into answers. He didn't push, but he didn't let it go either. He gave her space, the way he always did. The way he always had. And for a while, they talked around it. She sketched while he ranted. About work, about nothing, about things that didn't matter. But the hesitation she had carried all day settled, still sharp.

August's finger still absently traced the circle of his mug. It reminded her of something. It felt like... like she was standing before a massive sundial. Cracked stone, inlaid with bronze. Something familiar. Something she's seen before. She glanced at her drawing.

The anomaly stepped forward, testing the air with her toes. Sentinel had seen this before too, across multiple iterations. The gnomon, the blade which casts the shadow, was missing. The anomaly's fingers hovered just above the surface, hesitating, like touching it might reveal a truth she wasn't ready to hear.

"Katherine?" He said it. The name she had spent all day bracing herself against. It hit her harder than it should have, an impact somewhere deep in her ribs. She knew it didn't belong.

"What are you drawing? Can I see?"

"Don't," she said. The word was so quiet he almost didn't hear it. She flinched, barely enough. August caught it. The brief tightening of her shoulders, the way her fingers brushed against her sleeve before settling again.

His expression flattened from easy warmth to analytics. "Don't what? Did I miss something?"

The question, phrased like that, caught her off guard. She had spent years folding, adjusting, making herself fit. One more time wouldn't hurt. The world would keep moving. August would keep talking. And she would keep vanishing. *No. Not this time.*

"Don't call me that," she repeated. She still hadn't explained, but had trouble gathering the words. Her internal narration stopped. The urge to disappear constricted around her, an instinct from years of making herself smaller, of vanishing before she could be seen.

The anomaly would have regarded the panther. "My name is Sable," she said. The sundial reverberated. A verdict read before porcelain and brass. "Because a name is something that can't be taken. I am Sable, because I refuse to forget."

The glades were entirely indifferent to her choice, and the panther had grown tired of the spectacle of it all. The veil wouldn't have acknowledged it. Because to acknowledge a name is to acknowledge that it actually belonged to someone.

August sat his mug down, the ceramic against the wood table was a little too much. "Katherine? Why?"

Her breath steadied. She dropped the pencil and her eyes met his. They were defiant but also terrified. The name was waiting. The speech was prepared, but she lost it all in the quick glance into his eyes. "Because it's not my name. It never was. My name is Sable."

It held. August blinked. He didn't look hurt or angry, though she expected he might. He looked like he did when he couldn't figure out why a spreadsheet was returning the wrong output. *Error.*

She watched him mouth her name, silently. *Sable.* He let the name settle on his lips. It looked like a joke to her, though she knew it wasn't meant that way. He stopped tracing the rim of his mug. Just for a second. Then his finger resumed its rhythm, faster now, tapping instead of tracing.

The ground below her shifted. Something ancient receded for her. Her pulse pounded in her ears. She could take it back, laugh it off, let the moment slip past like she always did. But she didn't, because taking it back was more frightening than saying it in the first place.

On the page before her, the two slits of Sentinel's eyes watched her. She imagined they'd be... golden. Not yellow. Gold.

"Yeah," she said. "My middle name. It was the only thing that ever felt like mine. Before doctor's visits, college, and office life decided I was Katherine." Her voice was shaky. "Just Sable is fine."

She gave a short, startled laugh. It was almost apologetic. It caught in her throat. "That sounded dramatic."

August made eye contact. Perhaps for the first time in a while. His smile looked forced. Someone trying to appear calm while system warnings flashed in his vision. "A little.

You never told me before, so how was I supposed to know? I've been calling you the wrong name for…"

"Sorry." She shook her head and grasped his hand with both of hers. His tapping stopped. He radiated warmth. Pleasant to touch. She knew he cared for her. She probably felt the same toward him. A distant part of her expected the pressure that she'd carried to lift, even slightly. It didn't. Not exactly.

His expression stuttered, like he was seeing her for the first time, and didn't know how to. "Okay." He smiled again, but it didn't quite reach his eyes. She let go of his hand and he brought it back to his cup. The tapping didn't resume; it turned back to quiet circling instead. "Okay, Sable."

She glanced down at the drawing. At the panther who seemed to regard her without interest. He had been here long before the world had forgotten her. The panther sighed, and her skin interpreted it as prophecy. She didn't bother to ask if it was.

Sentinel regarded the anomaly. "Sable," he finally said. "They know you're here. The Edict will not look away."

She inhaled deeply, a steadier breath than she had taken in a long time. For a second, she waited for the dread to return. It didn't. The day wasn't over yet. She had said it, and nothing had collapsed. No resistance, no correction, no invisible force pressing her back into place. Only space, only air, only her. Yet the way he looked at her, a recalibration. A pattern rewritten in real time. What would it be like to fill the space she stood in?

Chapter 4

QUIET HAS DIFFERENT TEXTURES, depending on what it carries; sometimes, it can be heavy. Sometimes hostile. Sometimes the quiet of her apartment waited with eyes watching to see if she'd perform, even for herself. Sometimes it was like a mirror, held up in a way only she could see through. It was into this kind of quiet that Sable stepped. The city's noise, its movement, the weight of the workday; all of it remained beyond the door. It was like watching herself from the outside.

She sat her bag down, moving through the space with the same automatic precision she always did. Shoes off. Keys on the table. Coffee mug from this morning rinsed and left in the sink. Routine.

Then, she stopped at the edge of the counter. Her medication. She leaned against the surface, and let the thought settle into her ribs. The words danced in the air from earlier. *My name is Sable.*

She whispered it again, testing it. "Sable."

Her mind played it back over and over. A loop of narration. Her shoulders sagged at the strangeness of saying it aloud into a room that only watched. The name hung there. She let out a breath. Then, unexpectedly, laughed. She almost tried to correct it. Almost spoke an apology to the empty room, and then she laughed again at that notion. The static began to clear.

Her reflection in the kitchen window looked back at her, the city lights shimmering behind it. The glow caught the edges of her hair, turning the strands almost silver in places. She studied herself, searching for a difference, for some mark of change, but the reflection only stared back, distant. If she passed this face on the street tomorrow, would she recognize it as her own? She squinted. Tried to imagine what the unanswered would be doing right now.

The unanswered's chambers were cut from stone and sealed with porcelain. A world of sharp, precise mirrors. Even the shadows would be accounted for. Logged and categorized.

Only, one wall was different. Impossible. A faint ripple warped the far side of the chamber, revealing a single fracture in the mirrored truth. His hand rested just above the surface as his reflection stared back; its shoulders were softer, eyes less cold.

He hadn't slept. That was against protocol, too. He pressed his palm to the glass and a memory surfaced. Not a face or a name. A posture. A shape he once knew. He withdrew his hand, and the ripple remained.

She shrugged. Would this be when everything falls into place? Standing there, alone in her apartment, it was like listening for whispers in an empty cathedral. She wasn't sure if anything had changed at all.

Her eyes drifted to the drawer containing Penelope's letters. There were three. She didn't have to open the drawer to know. She had never thrown them away. Hadn't opened them in years. One of them, she had never opened. Not yet. The thought lingered, but she didn't reach for them.

She picked up the bottle from the bathroom counter, rolling it in her palm before shaking out a pill. She sat it back next to an old bottle of children's vitamins. She didn't look at it. But her fingers trembled, just enough.

The pill went down easily with a sip of water. It didn't change anything right away. But it was a choice. A good one.

She passed the bookshelf, where the tea Penelope left behind sat unopened. Earl Grey with something citrusy. Not her taste. But she never threw it away.

They'd called it grief-proofing. A joke, mostly. Buying things the other couldn't stand, just in case. So nothing would hurt too much if one of them disappeared. She'd laughed about it once when nobody else could hear her, because the idea was impossible to argue with.

She imagined the unanswered reaching up, touching his jaw, tracing the scar that bisected it.

He tapped it. Once. The contact startled him. Not the scar itself. What it was missing. The shape of the pain remained, but he couldn't remember the source. It was erased. Scraped clean.

She dragged a hand through her hair, strands catching between her fingers, the motion too practiced to soothe. A tightness gave, just enough. She flicked off the kitchen light and let the quiet have the room. Tomorrow, she'd say her name again. And she'd have to decide if she meant it.

Her dreams were rough. Oracles and decrees. They stood in a circle, faceless and tall. Their unity, once seamless, had begun to fray at the edges.

"We cut a thread," said the first oracle, "but its end hasn't been absorbed by the current yet."

"A single loose thread can unravel the entire design," intoned the second. Sharp. Final. "The faultline is a scar. A violation of the plane."

"The other threads now bend toward it," said the third. A hiccup in their cadence, as if testing the air between words. "She's listening."

They should have spoken as one. Now they splintered. A chorus broken into three distinct threads, each with their own texture. Even the echoes arrived late. Less certain of their place.

Morning came too soon. The office was still shaking off its sleep when Sable walked in. Light stretched across the desks and souls in uneven bands, catching on the edges of her glasses. Priya passed her, head turned too long before slipping away. Sable adjusted her posture, fingers grazing the desk, just to mark the spot.

There was no smile. No comment. A glance and nothing more. Her brain tried to find the pattern in it. Was it a question? A warning? An invitation of sorts? It probably didn't mean anything at all, but an idea began to form. That Sable might have wanted it to. The thought settled, the way one feels warmth even after the sun has moved. She didn't turn to meet it; but she didn't look away either.

The third oracle's body moved just after the others. A delay imperceptible to most, but not here in this sterile place. In this realm defined by precision, even the smallest deviation was glaring. The delay began to appear on the mirrored walls; glyphs above them searched for a category.

She sat at her desk, absently sketching. Her inbox was already filling with unread emails, but none of that seemed to matter. She was focused on something that mattered more. And then it happened. The subject line; *attendance encouraged*. Expected, was more accurate. Her fingers hovered over the mouse, but she didn't click.

The old pressure had settled in her chest, creeping upward. It would come soon. The question. The assumption. And she would have to decide.

A voice drifted in, effortless, routine. A coworker, Matthew. He brought a question that was not a question at all. "You're coming, right?"

She thought of her dream. Of the oracles. "She was meant to be erased," the first oracle intoned, like wind pressing against a window.

Her throat tightened. The word *yes* hovered, practiced and ready. Her body prepared for compliance. The nod. The automatic smile. The muscles in her cheek started to pull into that practiced mask. The words began forming before she could stop them. She could already hear herself saying yes, falling into the old choreography of invisibility.

"Meant? The term 'meant' is a fallacy of attribution," the second oracle countered. "There is only the pattern, and that which breaks it. She breaks it." The words severed. A click, a circuit closed.

She had spent years saying *yes*. Too many times. To Katherine. To expectation. To everything except herself. Matthew furrowed his brow. He was dissecting her.

The third oracle froze out of sequence. The words formed, a counter-resonance, sharp and clear. "Why is she here?"

"I need to..." Her voice stuck. The excuse didn't come. She knew she didn't need one, and yet she searched anyway.

"To not."

That made no sense. And it was also the most true thing she could say. She almost laughed. Almost cried. Her mind scrambled for an excuse but came up with only static and disjointed action.

The unanswered's hand drifted to the sword at his side. The sword was an object that was more symbol than weapon. Forged to correct. Still, it had remained undisturbed since his return from the faultline. Now, his fingers curled around its hilt, and the metal hummed against his skin, threatening to wake. The Edict's decree had already begun to stir within it.

Matthew blinked. He gave a half smile. Either sympathy or amusement. She wasn't sure. Then he nodded and turned away. As if she hadn't just ruptured the veil. As if her imaginary construct hadn't just accepted the order to kill her. To erase the anomaly. To try again. And again. Until the end of fucking time. To keep pressing her until she vanished.

But nothing cracked. The ceiling held. The room absorbed her refusal like any other sound. Keyboards clicked, low conversations rising and fading. No ripple. No reaction. Quiet, settling like dust. The room began rewriting itself, but no one else seemed to mark the change.

Her chest loosened; the pressure stayed, but it no longer pinned her. She didn't know what came next, and for once, that was okay. More choices, surely. But today, this one held.

She had always noticed the texture of noise. And while there were countless kinds of silence, there were really only two kinds of noise; the kind she could slip into, like a frayed coat sleeve, and the kind that unmoored her bones. But this noise didn't make her want to vanish; even though her heart beat louder than the printer's hum, and the keyboards clicked along like a river moving without her.

She glanced down at the sketch she had been working on before Matthew arrived. The unanswered, watching his own reflection. Only, it didn't follow him. One version of him remained behind. His head slightly tilted. Eyes searching. A ripple locked in graphite. He didn't look away.

Around her, the atmosphere of the office folded inward, taut. It waited for an answer to a question she dared not ask.

Chapter 5

THE RESEARCH WING WAS still waking up. The fluorescents buzzed overhead, cold, casting everything in an artificial glow. The hum of a distant printer punctuated the silence, papers sliding into the tray like the turning of gears. Outside, the city was alive, but here, the world was held in suspension.

Sable stepped inside, her coat wrapped around her shoulders, the worn fabric pulling against her arms as she clutched it close. The sharp bite of the air-conditioning cut through her skin. She let the cold settle; it kept her alert, grounded.

Her bag landed on the desk with practiced ease. The motions were instinctual, a choreography repeated until it barely registered, yet the day pressed differently beneath the surface of routine. Her fingers gripped her company ID badge, clipped neatly to her lanyard. The plastic caught the overhead light, throwing back a name that didn't belong to her anymore.

Across the room, the self-service kiosk in front of the HR desk hummed in expectation, its small screen glowing with a waiting prompt. *NAME FOR BADGE PRINT-ING.* Sable stepped forward. A weight settled low in her calves. Not fear. Fear scatters. This pulled inward, like gravity remembering itself.

Her fingers hovered over the keyboard for only a breath. Then, she typed: *Sable Mercier.*

The man beyond the HR counter gave her a pleasant look. He didn't mean it. She took the slip of paper and her old ID badge from the machine and carefully passed it to him. Her fingers trembled as she offered a piece of herself. She forced her hand to be still and clenched her jaw tightly.

He didn't pause to ask, *Are you sure?* He looked everything over, twice. And then, "New preferred name?"

Her jaw loosened. Just enough. "My middle name." He wasn't entitled to an explanation. She had given it anyway. Automatic.

He didn't sigh, probably. Instead, he turned around without another word. The room stared back at her. No alarms, no correction, no rejection. He had walked away, presumably to print her new badge. But now she stood there, grappling with the act itself. Choosing to live in a place that defied the pattern prescribed. A panic swept over her. What if he returned? Told her that it wasn't allowed. That she'd need more forms. Management approval. Perhaps some external proof to verify the decision. Her mind drifted, held in this thought.

The tight cubicles had arranged themselves like trees, leaning close and too still, the gray fabric walls as bark.

Ethernet cables had stitched together to form branches, soaked in mist; their roots coiled like muscle through damp, yielding soil.

The anomaly stepped forward, her fists already clenched without meaning to. The ground groaned beneath each step. Loose packed but unwilling to settle. Her cloak dragged through the mist, frayed and not fully formed.

"The forest won't remember you." Sentinel's voice barely rippled. Flat and observational.

The man from HR cleared his throat. She blinked, composing herself. She gave a sheepish smile, which he returned. He slid the new badge across the counter. The old one had a hole punched through it. She held the new badge in front of her. Warm plastic, freshly stamped. Real.

"Now accepting name changes from ghosts and dissidents," she muttered to herself.

"Sorry?" A puzzled look.

"Oh, nothing," she added, cheeks turning a bit red.

She looked over her shoulder, but the open floor of the research wing looked entirely disinterested in her new badge. There was no panther or guide, only a canopy of fluorescents and stained ceiling tiles. *Why are you hiding in there?* She thought. She aimed the question at the nearest cubicle. To the trunk of the nearest tree. As if daring it to respond. But the office had no tolerance for her noise or her imagination. You can't imagine yourself out of your problems, or your anxieties. But sometimes, her dreams cast the world in a light that was less harsh. It made the texture of her surroundings less abrasive. More kind. Or at least, more interesting.

Her fingers pressed into the badge's warmth, tracing the newly formed letters. Letters that held a restrained kind of promise. She waited for resistance; for the world to push back.

No one rushed over to tell her she had made a mistake. The veil did not reach her. Her fingers closed around the badge, sliding it into place over the old one, the one with the hole punched through its center, sealing the warm card between layers of smooth plastic and burying the old behind it.

"You are like a child in a graveyard." Sentinel's raspy voice echoed in her mind. "Picking up bones you don't understand. Be careful what you touch. Not everything is kind. Not everything is meant for you to take."

But what did he know? Not everything. He couldn't know everything. The stiffness behind her neck settled, though still heavier than it should have been. But not pressing, at least. A counter-balance.

Low conversation flickered around the meeting room, half-formed and forgettable. It barely cleared the threshold of notice. The meeting began with the dry click of a remote signaling the changing slides. This was louder. Information moved across the screen in clean bullet points. Dr.

Harlan stood at the front, leading the meeting with his usual efficiency.

Sable sat near the back, her badge cool against her chest. She brushed her thumb along the edges, tracing the raised letters beneath the plastic film. Usually, being seen hit her bones first. Sharp, electric, inescapable. But there was no crawl beneath her jawbone, no scorch behind her eyes. She was unarmed, but for once that recognition didn't feel like exposure.

Dr.□Harlan didn't glance up from the slide deck. "Katherine, you own the Q2 heart-failure readmission dashboard."

A hostile silence. Not pause; blade.

"Yes." The word was steady.

He advanced the slide. A bar graph flickered. 18□% in red. Someone shifted in their chair. A pen clicked.

She held her expression neutral, careful; a steadiness that masked an undercurrent she refused to reveal.

"This spike doesn't match Q1. Re-extract the data, make sure we're still indexing on primary discharge, and strip any transfer cases like before. Refresh by Friday."

A moment. A tremor of something in Dr. Harlan's face. His gaze lingered for a fraction too long, as if catching an inconsistency in her that he couldn't quite name. Did he notice?

Then, she gave a nod. Simple. Unquestioning. Some burdens were meant to be screamed into pillows until the sound was lost. To pick this one up now would be to make it hers. She let it go.

The meeting moved on. Conversation resumed. The air had grown heavier. Each breath required more effort than the last. Matthew leaned over, voice low but assured. "I rewrote your SQL join. There were duplicate MRNs in the final table."

She blinked. *Duplicates?* What duplicates? Her report had no errors. She was sure of it. She studied the report again, and the structure was different. Rewritten. Changed. Every data pull is logged. Matthew's 'fix' means a new audit trail entry with his name, instead of hers. She could have said something. She should have said something. Instead, she nodded.

No one called her silence a resistance, or cowardice. It was anticipated. Expected. The moment passed with surgical neatness. Some pauses drew suspicion. Hers never had. It was safe.

Her eyes found the change log. The original script now had Matthew's name on it. His commit message taunted her: *bug fix.*

Dr. Harlan sat down and flipped through the report in front of him, shaking his head slightly. "The Q2 data isn't lining up. It's just not credible," he said, more to the room at large rather than directly. "Something's getting tangled in the data pull. It's downstream noise, and it's making the whole forecast unusable. It looks like a cell was shifted, maybe? It's throwing all the rest of the data off."

A problem was presented without an owner, which made it everyone's problem, but especially Sable's. This was her dashboard, and she knew hers was right. She started to open her mouth, but before sound could form, Matthew spoke first.

"You know, I think I see the issue," Matthew said. His tone was easy, confident. A gentle discovery. He reached out to the report in front of her, but he spoke to the room. Flipped a page, then another. Stabbed a line with his finger. "It's a super common mistake. I think it's pulling from legacy rollover or transfer cases."

That was most certainly not the issue. Matthew had copied and pasted entire columns, trying to style up the formatting and he brought the discrepancy himself.

Matthew looked up at Dr. Harlan. "I can write a quick patch script to clean that up, if you'd like."

He glanced at Sable, as if he was asking for her permission. She knew he wasn't. Harlan nodded, already moving on.

A patch script wouldn't fix this. The dataset needed to be rerun from the original pull. She tried, once, to correct. "Actually, I..."

But someone talked over her, a voice severing hers mid-thought. The opportunity dissolved.

She tried again. "That's not..." But it came out only as a whisper, and Dr. Harlan had already moved on. He didn't even hear her.

Priya watched. Her lips parted like she might speak, but she didn't. Sable didn't blame her; this wasn't Priya's fire to walk into. No one remembered this moment except Sable.

Later, the office moved around her, the distant hum of conversation blending into the mechanical rhythm of keyboards and the occasional ring of a phone. Papers shuffled. A chair scraped against the floor.

No one looked at her. No one saw her pressing her fingers into her desk. It was solid, but well worn from years of absent-minded gestures like this. Her nails dug in, slightly. Enough to feel the pressure. Enough to remind herself that she was here. She studied the grooves in the edge of the desk. The scene unfolded there. Branches parted. A figure emerged, tall and cloaked in the shadows of the world's law. His jacket trailed through mist like an unclaimed memory. The unanswered. He didn't speak. He didn't need to. They both knew what he had come for.

Fuck Matthew, she thought. She blinked, cracked her neck and smoothed away the scene from her imagination. Thinking it wasn't as satisfying as saying it. But she had work to do, even if it would be overwritten later. Her report was gone. It was theft, but the subtle warmth of the badge at her fingertips remained. It mattered. That this, at least, was still hers.

The break room hummed with quiet chaos. Coffee sticks stirring, discarded without care. A chorus of conversations. None for her. A hiccup in data integrity was the hot gossip of the week. She hadn't revisited the meeting in thought. Only in sensation. Tracing moments like scrapes and lumps.

She went to sip her coffee but missed her mouth slightly, a tremble in her wrist she didn't expect. A splash hit her collarbone. She wiped it off without comment, but her cheeks flushed.

The door swung open behind her. Priya walked in, drawn to the familiar corner ritual. Sugar packets rustled. A spoon stirred, metal on ceramic. Then, Priya slowed. Her eyes flicked to the badge, then back to Sable's face; a corner of her mouth quirked up.

"Sable," she said, nodding once. "I was just gonna ask you if you saw that email from HR about the symmetry retreat. Sounds like my personal hell."

Sable blinked, softened. Priya had just used her name, her real name, as a simple entry to office gossip.

"I... yeah, I saw it," Sable stammered. "I hate it so much."

She turned slightly. Priya's eyes flicked to the badge again, briefly, like she was testing how it fit before deciding. Then, as if there was never a question, Priya nodded.

"I was planning to have a 'scheduling conflict,'" Priya said.

"Good call," Sable said.

But she was somewhere else. *Oh, you don't want me calling you by the name your mother says when you're in trouble? Fine, Sable it is.* Said years ago, in a car, in laughter. She hadn't thought about that night with Penelope in forever. A breath left her, slower, steadier than before. Priya had spoken her name as though it had always belonged to her.

"It's my middle name." It was the easiest answer to a question Priya never asked. The least intrusive. Though a part of her wanted Priya to dig deeper. Penelope would have said, *That's bullshit. My middle name is Herminia, and I hate it. Everyone hates their middle name.*

But Priya simply lifted her cup to her lips. "Okay," she said. "You didn't need a reason, though."

She didn't question it further. She didn't make it a conversation. She accepted it. Like it was the easiest thing in the world. Sable wrapped her hands around the coffee cup, letting the warmth soak into her palms. No pushback. No hesitation. Just acceptance.

The conversation slid deeper into office gossip, who was dating who, a minor complaint about overnight lab results. Nothing important. But something had changed. She was speaking more freely. The words came easier. The space between them wasn't as tense, no longer waiting for her to explain herself. She was talking to someone as Sable.

Priya drained the last of her cup and stood, stretching. She made for the door, then tilted her head, as if reconsidering.

"See you later, Sable."

Not Katherine. Not a question. Just a name. Sable watched her go, then traced the letters on her badge, feeling the raised edges of her name beneath her grasp. It didn't feel borrowed.

She glanced up at the ceiling. Imagined the third oracle there, watching. They should have intervened. The Edict would have demanded it. But they watched.

Something stirred within them. Something unsanctioned. Something like doubt. The third oracle didn't understand yet, but they remembered the shape of understanding. And it made them want to scream or laugh or cry. Absurd.

Sable let go of a tension she hadn't realized she was holding. Then, she walked back to her desk. She sat down and began scrolling through her inbox. The unread emails were all addressed to Katherine. The name didn't sting, but it didn't sit right, either. It remained a line on a screen, belonging to someone else.

She didn't correct them or resent them. But the absence settled deeper than she expected. It was an ache in her joints. Something taken, leaving behind a feeling that she couldn't shake.

The anomaly didn't watch the blade held to her throat. She watched him. The construct, the antagonist, the unanswered.

"It won't work," she told him. "It's just noise right? You can't calculate your way out of a bad memory. Not when the noise is you."

She offered her throat to the blade, crowding it. Daring him to follow through. He blinked. Twice. The second time with recognition. Something once lost. A trace of warmth that hadn't been programmed. "My function," he stammered. "Was not to choose. I'm breaking. I... I can't break."

Her fingers hovered over the mouse, then opened the data-warehouse audit log, tagged her original query, *superseded without QC review,* and clicked save. It wouldn't stop the rollout, but it planted a timestamp. Evidence she was here.

Priya had called her Sable. Priya had said it like it was hers. Her hands hovered over the keyboard, resting. She watched the cursor blink in an empty email draft. Her own name was missing from the work she did, but there it was, in the signature of a new email. *Katherine Mercier.* A name for someone who disappeared. A name that was easier to carry when she needed to be no one at all. Tomorrow, she will wear the new badge again.

Chapter 6

Keyboard clicks. Unintelligible chatter. The rustle of paper like leaves. The office rested in its rhythm. If it weren't for the awful lights, she might have found peace here.

Sable sat at her desk, her screen glowing with numbers and reports, her fingers poised over the keyboard. A formula, a task, something structured.

It was all too easy. Numbers had always balanced for her, like a second language. She could manipulate variables like paint on a canvas. Symmetry among chaos. She took a breath, flipped her sketchbook back over and turned a page. She thought of the oracles, and began sketching.

The silence in the citadel was unkind. The thin, hollow silence of a machine slipping its gears. The glyphs that once spiraled in haunting arcs now grew faint. Some drifted, unmoored, leaving dark streaks across the mirrored walls. Walls which shifted erratically, highlighting recent divergences.

The third oracle hovered out of formation. She sketched it off-center. Their glow was off-phase, their motion half a breath out of time. The change would have been imperceptible to most. But here, in a chamber of harsh fluorescent lights and tuned to unbroken rhythm, even a momentary hesitation was a fracture.

A voice called her out of the daydream. She barely registered it at first. Priya.

"Hey, Sable," she had said, leaning against the side of the desk, coffee in hand, scrolling through her phone. Preoccupied, but here.

"Oh, Priya. Sorry you startled me a little."

Priya gave no indication that she heard the apology. Her eyes scanned her phone instead. Her expression was unchanged. "There's this art exhibit opening this weekend, and a 2 for 1 discount on tickets. You'd probably like it."

The words sounded light, but they settled somewhere deeper. She blinked. Would she? She used to. Her first instinct was to deflect. A polite *maybe*, a noncommittal *we'll see*. The answer that keeps things simple.

"Yeah," Sable said, surprising herself. The words left her before she could reconsider them, too late to take them back. "I'd like to go."

Priya glanced up. The answer didn't surprise her; the ease did. She nodded once, approving. "Good, I'll send you the details. It's a pop-up, I think it runs all month. I can't make it this weekend. Wife and I are planting some trees in the backyard. She's got the green thumb, I'm only there for moral support, but you should go."

A ripple ran through Sable's thoughts. Something caught. Words intended to be internal formed quietly on her lips. "Oh. Me and August. Right."

Priya tilted her head.

"Nothing," Sable said quickly. "It just sounded like… Nevermind."

Priya smiled, a little apologetic. "Next time. Promise." She glanced back at her phone before continuing. "Cool. I'll text you. You should take August, it would be good for you both."

She tapped a note into her phone and moved on. No questions. No second glance. No expectation. Sable glanced at her drawing.

"Your place was empty," the first oracle intoned. The sound emerged as a resonance, a vibration shared through charged air. "Where did you linger?"

"They flicker," the second oracle cut in, forgoing subtlety. "The signature is precise. Whose unraveling did you touch?"

The third oracle let the silence stretch. Intentional. They weren't weighing what response to give. They weren't sure the questions deserved a response at all.

Finally, they spoke. A low hum, directed inward more than to the others. "I was observing a failure in one of our instruments," they said. "It seemed… significant."

A thread of possibility curled through the sterility of the office. It offered no pressure, only a choice. She looked back at her screen. The data was there. The room pressed the same as before, but her breathing had become easier.

Later, the apartment held its hush, and the city pressed faintly against the glass. Beyond, headlights blurred into streaks, slipping past as if measuring time with arcs of light. Inside, the warm glow of a campfire-bulbed lamp spilled over the coffee table, casting uneven shadows that wavered across the floor.

Sable sat on the couch, her phone resting on her knee. The screen was already open, the number waiting. She had never deleted it.

She almost closed the app. Almost let it fade like she had a dozen times before.

"What's the point?" she muttered.

Her thumb hovered over the screen. It would be so easy to close the app. To put the phone away. To pretend she had never considered calling. But she had considered it. She was considering it. She pressed the button.

The ringing reverberated sharper in the quiet of her apartment. She felt it in her feet more than her ear. Once. Twice. She considered hanging up. She picked up a pencil and began scratching it against the back of the envelope in front of her.

The third oracle turned inward. A pressure building to- ward action. They reached. A question shaped into something that might register. Not contagious… inviting. They injected it into the shared space between the other two oracles.

On the other end of the line, a voice. "Sable?"

Not Katherine. Just certainty. The tension in her ribs unraveled, thread by thread. Momentarily, she gripped the phone tighter, as if holding onto the moment. She swallowed, and the space between them held like static, charged and waiting.

"Yeah. Hey."

The words sounded strange, like a language she hadn't spoken in years but still understood. Penelope laughed, warm and familiar, like she was saving a seat Sable had forgotten was hers.

"God, it's been forever. Are you… wait, are you calling just to say hi?"

Sable hesitated. Just long enough for Penelope to hear it.

"I don't know. Maybe."

Penelope paused. Gears shifted, turning and aligning into place. Then, Penelope's voice got very flat, very clear. "Okay. What happened?"

"What do you mean?"

"I mean, you don't call just to say hi. Not after this long. So what happened? Did August propose? Did someone at work try to 'helpfully' explain your own job to you again? Give me the headline."

Another pause.

"Alright. Give me the coordinates. Where are you right now, in your head?"

The questions were almost careless in how easily they were asked, but they landed like a fingertip pressed to a bruise Sable had learned to ignore. And then the last one. It was the kind of question no one at work would ask. No one meant harm. Just, nobody bothered to ask things like this. Katherine didn't need checking on. Katherine was fine.

She didn't answer right away. Instead, she ran her palm along the rough seam of the envelope. Tried not to imagine the feel of her empty hand closing on itself.

"I'm getting there," she said, her voice flatter than normal.

Silence on the other end. Then Penelope's voice, devoid of all sympathy and therefore full of respect. "Getting where, Sable? 'There' isn't a destination. Are you closer to yourself than you were yesterday? Yes or no."

The question was a punch, clean and direct. It didn't ask her to measure progress against some imaginary finish line. It asked for a single data point. Yesterday versus now. Manageable. Real.

Query: If the pattern is perfect, an anomaly cannot exist. If an anomaly exists, is the pattern imperfect? If that pattern is imperfect, is correction a flaw?

The two other oracles rejected it, cleanly.

Sable's breath hitched. The warm plastic of the new name badge. The words she could have said to Dr. Harlan.

Could have said, but didn't. Leaving the feedback form blank. The porcelain path ahead curved.

"...Yes," she whispered.

"Okay," Penelope said, and the relief in her voice was a sharp exhale. "Okay. That's a heading. That's something we can work with. Next question... What tools are you using?"

That was how they talked after that. Not about old stories and forgotten moments. That was nostalgia, and nostalgia was a trap. This was triage. Penelope didn't ask *Are you painting again?* That's a yes/no question that invites shame. She asked, "Have you seen your sketchbook lately? Is it still in the house?"

Sable's fingers tightened around the pencil. A reflex. "It's... around."

"Good," Penelope said, her voice final. "Then it's still a tool you can pick up. You don't have to use it. Just know where it is."

The third oracle tried again to query the other two. This time, not a logical claim. A memory. A series of impossible sensations. The feeling of a hand closing around another's. The scent of popcorn, mostly spilled on the bedroom floor. A laugh. A gesture that didn't need to be defined.

When the call ended, Sable didn't feel warm. She didn't feel comforted, either. She felt... seen. Like someone had just walked into her dark, messy room, ignored the chaos, and handed her a flashlight and a fresh set of batteries.

Evening settled in deeper. Outside, the city breathed, distant sirens, muffled conversations, footsteps settling against wet pavement. A world continuing beyond these walls.

She disturbed a book on the shelf. Then another. Searching without knowing whether she would find it. And then, her fingers brushed against something unexpected, though it shouldn't have been. A sketchbook. Worn, edges softened from time. The cover was rough beneath her fingertips.

She froze, as if she had been the one found. Like the sketchbook itself had been searching, rummaging past discarded things until brushing a curtain aside and seeing her face. Her hands trembled, the book halfway back to the shelf, caught.

"It's just paper," she muttered.

The pages were stiff with time, the scent of old charcoal rose as she opened the book. Dark lines. Quick strokes of ink. Unfinished ideas. A sketch of a figure, soft, deliberate, coat trailing behind him. Her own hands, drawn from memory. An alien landscape, lines bold and erratic. A self-portrait, the eyes unfinished, left empty, waiting.

She listened, as if something had stirred within it, or within her, but not yet found its place. She had let this part of herself fade, convinced it no longer held meaning.

But now, with charcoal beneath her fingertips, she saw the truth. This was never forgotten; only waiting.

Her fingers traced the rough texture of the charcoal. The smudges left behind. The evidence that she was here. That she created. She flipped the page, and there, tucked between the sheets, was an old ticket stub. Faded ink barely legible, a gallery opening. Years ago.

The third oracle reached for something. A thread of memory, nestled beside glyphs that no longer spoke. It carried the echo of another world, marked so it could only be found when it was unbearable not to. They didn't place it so much as anchor it, folded into a place where memory held form only when chosen. It was left for her.

She had gone with Penelope to the gallery. They'd split a bottle of cheap wine in paper cups beforehand.

She remembered it. The smell of the paint. The low hum of conversation. The way Penelope had stood too long in front of one painting before declaring, "It's a beautiful, fucking lie, isn't it."

Sable's grip tightened around the stub. She smiled, barely. Then folded the memory away. For the first time, she considered picking up charcoal, imagining the weight of it in her hand, the tactile familiarity, a connection rekindled through sensation rather than thought.

She woke before the city, and with her a quiet hope. The urgency of the day hadn't settled in yet. Traffic crawled past her as she walked, the usual clatter of morning routines beginning like clockwork set in motion. The sky was muted, the light filtered through thin clouds.

The bell above the café door chimed as Sable stepped inside. The scent of fresh coffee greeted her immediately, bright and citrusy, roasted with something floral. Conversations ebbed and pooled between the tables.

She ordered her drink, and when the barista asked her name, she said, "Sable." Like it meant something.

Hearing the name spoken aloud when her drink was ready landed softer than she expected. But something in her posture shifted, like she wasn't sure if someone might be watching. As if they were wondering whether she had the right.

She turned slightly, her body angling toward the door, ready to leave, until she stopped. There was an empty table by the window. A perfect view of the street. The kind of place she might have chosen once, a long time ago.

The chair's surface was cool beneath her fingertips. A small detail, but it mattered. She pulled out the art book she bought days ago, the pages crisp, unblemished. She flipped to a section on color theory, contrast, saturation, depth. Concepts that once came instinctually, naturally.

A language she understood. She traced a diagram with her fingertip, mapping the flow of warm tones into cool ones, the way color can transform space. She sipped her coffee as a page turned. The page became a chamber within the citadel. The third oracle hovered there, slightly off-center.

Their form unraveled at the seams. A flaw, perhaps. Or the beginning of form. The desire to peel themselves off the paper and breathe real air.

"She should not be alone," they whispered. To the chamber? To themself. The words drifted to her, though. It was the kind of sentence spoken in the dark, to a friend who once sat beside you on the floor of a childhood home. A sentence shaped like loyalty. Somewhere within the Loom, the relentless spinning pattern faltered. Then it began to weave a new design.

Penelope had once told her that color theory was just emotion dressed up in a lab coat. She hadn't thought about that in years.

Outside, the city continued. This time, she was not watching from the edges. She was within it; breathing alongside it, not apart. An unbroken stream of people strolled past, just beyond the glass, and for once, she didn't need to pull away. She belonged here.

Chapter 7

THE ART EXHIBIT HUMMED. Murmurs intertwined with footsteps absorbed by polished floors. They were punctuated now and then by distant laughter. Slanted beams of light filtered in from high windows, crafting small shadows across the cool marble. The air was light, tinged with the scent of aged paint and a whisper of something metallic, like time lingering in the room.

Sable moved through the space with August, their steps measured, unrushed. The coat was loose around her shoulders. It didn't feel heavy today. Just present. Warm in a way that made her feel slightly less opaque.

She stopped before a painting, abstract, intricately layered, chaotic yet purposeful. Each brushstroke was a deliberate echo of emotion left unanswered. It held her. Her fingers pressed into the fabric in her coat pocket, searching.

August stepped beside her.

"It's interesting," he said, tilting his head. "The composition's unbalanced, but there's a rhythm to it. Like it's meant to keep the eye moving."

His voice was thoughtful, considering it carefully, more analysis than feeling. Sable heard him, but the words were separate from what she was experiencing. His voice was low, but the painting was loud. She wasn't analyzing it. She was walking through it. They were looking at the same thing. But only one of them had ever had to hold themselves still enough not to be read wrong.

The brushstrokes pulled at her, streaks of color colliding and merging. They spoke in a way she understood. She let the painting settle in her chest. She glanced briefly at August as he stepped away. She held something that she hadn't fully realized she needed. Space to explore without explanation.

The first thing Sable noticed was the wind. A thin, hollow whistle. The trees became sparse. Beyond them, *what*? The observatory emerged on the canvas, as if from fog. Like a thought remembered on the way to forgetting. Her eyes traced the dome. It was split open to a sky without stars. Its once-pristine arches bent inward, warped by neglect and the slow abrasion of time. What remained of its structure leaned at impossible angles, as though reality itself had grown tired of supporting it.

She almost said something, about the pull of the colors, about the way they pressed into each other yet never fully merged. *It feels like...* The words formed on her tongue, but they caught before she could say them aloud. August was still analyzing. Breaking it apart into balance and movement and composition. If she said it, he would hear her, but he wouldn't understand. So she let the moment pass.

His sweater looked warm. She wanted to touch it. Wanted to wrap her fingers through it and breathe it in. An urge rose within her to slip her hand into his. To find an anchor in him. But his arms stayed crossed, expression thoughtful. She left her hand in her pocket. The space between them... the faultline, the word forming, began to widen. A question that she chose not to answer.

After the exhibit, they kissed briefly and he went off to run some errands. She released what she hadn't yet named, letting the tenderness of the exhibit shape her next steps as she moved toward the optical shop.

The shop was the kind that makes everything feel dull, a little more forgiving. Shelves lined with frames stretched along the walls, small mirrors catching fragments of movement, people trying on new identities, discarding old ones.

Sable stood before a display, her fingers brushing lightly over the edge of a pair of glasses. They were round, modern. Different from the thin wire frames she was used to. She lifted them. The heft in her hands was unfamiliar, but not wrong.

A voice drifted from behind the counter. "You've been away a while."

Sable looked up. The optician remembered her. A dozen explanations and thoughts flickered through her mind, why she never came back, why her prescription has likely changed, why this place feels different than before. But she didn't offer one.

"Yeah. It's been a while."

The optician nodded, as if that's all that needs to be said.

She tried on the glasses. She saw herself, clear and sharp. She didn't compare. She didn't search for what was different before. It was her. Here. Now. Steady and undeniable. Had she expected to see something else, someone else? Her reflection framed her in a way the glasses alone didn't explain.

"They suit you."

The words settled. It didn't feel like permission or validation. It was truth.

"I'll take them."

She left the shop, tucking the receipt into her bag. Her new glasses would arrive in about a week. Penelope's voice, dry and knowing, echoed in her mind. "People change their look and then they act different. Like we can't see the same person underneath."

Sable had rolled her eyes at the time. Now, she wasn't so sure. The thought stayed, carrying her into the warm hum of the bar. To Priya.

The bar was understated; polished wood, faded mirrors, and a richness in the atmosphere. Citrus, smoke, and old varnish. Conversations blended into a rhythm beneath the occasional clink of glassware and the dry scrape of chairs shifting against the scuffed floor.

They sat near the window, Sable's glass resting in front of her, undrank. Outside, neon signs flickered against the buildings, painting the city in restless color. Across from her, Priya watched. She was leaning back, the stool under her creaking.

"Still wearing the coat, huh?"

Sable glanced down, fingertips lightly tracing the frayed edge of the cuff.

"Yeah. It's comfortable."

Priya smirked, taking a sip of her drink. Her nail flicked the glass once. She didn't press.

The conversation drifted to office gossip, small frustrations, that sort of thing. Sable followed, kept up even. Rather than observing the conversation from the aisle, she was almost present. The distance collapsed. Like she was sitting in the chair beside herself rather than watching from far away. She was close. Closer than usual. She laughed, more a giggle really. And for the briefest moment, Sable looked across the table at Priya, from her own eyes. Her own chair.

Priya studied her, tilting her head slightly. She was considering not just what Sable had been saying, but how she held the words. *Had she noticed?*

"You seem different lately."

Sable didn't look away. She didn't deflect, but she did drift slightly. Not to the side. Further back. Her fingers grasped the edge of the table, a tether for her focus. "I think I am," she said. If she lost grip of the table, she might fall out of her chair, through the floor. She might crash through every level of the hollow spire, and never find herself again.

"Do you ever feel like..." Sable paused. She could feel the words forming before she had determined whether they were acceptable for public consumption. "Like you're speaking with a delay? Like everyone else is on a live broadcast, and you're on a seven-second tape delay, so when you finally talk, the conversation has already moved on? And you just... stand there, with the words still in your mouth? Only then there's times where it just all comes out at once, like now, and you might just say something you didn't mean. Or you did mean, but didn't mean to mean it."

The words hung there. It wasn't that Priya's expression had become unreadable. Sable had simply turned inward, and was now trying to justify. To backtrack. "Or maybe I'm just tired of translating myself."

Priya's body stilled, then leaned forward almost imperceptibly. She sat her drink down. A soft thud ricocheted through Sable's elbows. "Translating?" she asked, her nose scrunching up.

Sable looked away. Down. "Myself. Translating myself. To... everyone. I mean..." She shook her head, frustrated.

She still didn't look back at her face. She was barely holding onto the railing within the spire. If she made eye contact, she'd slip entirely. She stared at Priya's sleeve instead. It was crisp. She wanted to touch it. "People just look at you," she went on. "That look. Like you're... a glitch. Too much? Not enough? Nobody's ever told me which one it is."

Her fingers wrapped around the base of the glass, steadying her breath. "It's like being translated badly. All the time."

"Anyway," she said lightly, "I just used to think this was my fault." She risked a glance up to Priya's hairline.

Priya tilted her head, the corner of her mouth twitching with something that wasn't amusement. She traced the condensation circle on the table from where her drink had been.

"Oh, I know that one," she said. "Shit, figuring out it was the rest of the world that was the problem and not me? I was 25 before I figured that out."

"It's exhausting," Sable admitted. "Trying to show up."

"Yeah," Priya said. "And they don't exactly hand out promotions for being messy." She took another drink. "Especially when..."

She let the sentence hang, unfinished. It sat between them. Sable tried to finish the sentence in her own mind. But now it was Priya who was looking elsewhere, down. At her own hands. Nothing came. Sable kept watching Priya's hands. "You ever get tired of people assuming they understand you after five minutes?" she asked.

"Only every week," Priya replied. The pad of her hand absently slid through the ring of condensation on the table as she leaned forward, eyes looking right through her. She didn't seem to notice that her sleeve was damp now. "I'm Brown. And I'm Queer. It's like the world skims the headline and decides it's read the whole book."

Sable laughed. It emerged awkwardly. She clenched the hem of her coat. "Yeah. That."

"My mom always said I was too loud to be lovable. I spent a decade learning how to be quiet and still didn't get invited to things." Priya leaned back, exhausted. "People are lazy. You're just used to people not trying."

Sable's lips twitched, the echo of a complicated feeling. "Maybe. I don't even know what trying looks like, most days."

Priya tapped the table between their glasses. The vibration shot through Sable's elbows. "It looks like this," Priya said simply. "You showed up. We're talking. Stop footnoting everything."

The city outside blurred into ribbons of color. For once, the noise didn't feel like pressure. Just something to brace against.

She said nothing. And that was a choice.

The words hung for a breath too long. She took a sip, the chill of the glass catching her teeth. "Sorry," Sable said. "That all sounded... dramatic."

Priya didn't flinch. "Sable, my entire family communicates in drama. My nani's having an affair. And my Mom, she still thinks I'm a receptionist. This is barely an appetizer. You're fine."

A small smile. Sable shifted her stool, her shoulders lowered, enough. That's all.

They kept talking, their voices weaving between the background noise. For a second, she almost reached for her phone. An instinct. A tether. But instead, she pressed her fingers into the glass, feeling the cold. Sable lifted her drink, taking another sip. For once, she didn't feel out of place.

The comfort of the conversation followed her home, weaving into the apartment, the city's distant hum carrying a question that she didn't know how to ask yet.

The apartment windows held back the world long enough for that question to emerge. A curiosity that reached with trembling fingers and a crack in its voice.

There were two boxes at the top of the closet. A shoebox, taped shut with filament and rage. And the moving box. They each held a version of her. An old one. And a forgotten one. She reached, slid the moving box down. Was she ready? She eased the lid open. The past settled in. Some things stayed in the dark because they were meant to be forgotten. Some stayed because she hadn't decided what to do with them.

She sat on the floor, cross-legged. The box was open, but in her mind's eye... she was at the threshold of the observatory.

Sable followed the pull, her hand brushing against a cracked panel as she passed beneath another archway. She ran her fingers through the dust on its surface and instantly tasted its grit at the back of her throat.

She found a notebook, creased and worn. Lists. Goals. Notes written in a version of her handwriting that felt distant, foreign. A conference name tag from years ago. The name Katherine, printed in bold. Sentinel would have stood on a high ledge near the open dome, his eyes turned upward into the void where stars should be. She would have approached, each step feeling like she was claiming the floor. But as she drew near, he kept his eyes up, and away from hers.

"You've seen this place before. It's real isn't it?" Her voice was fragile, seeking an anchor.

The panther's head tilted, a barely perceptible motion against the starless void. "A better question," he rumbled, his voice like distant thunder, "is why you need it to be."

She lifted a framed award from the box, the glass slightly dusty. Recognition for something she once worked toward, something that once mattered. *Katherine Sable Mercier.* So official. It was heavier than she remembered. She could keep it. She could throw it away. Either choice meant something, and she wasn't sure which truth she was ready to hold. She gripped the name tag, fingers tight around the plastic. She almost tossed it into the trash, but stopped. Some endings were just too sharp to touch, and that had nothing to do with nostalgia or grief.

She regarded the panther again. "Then tell me what happened here," she demanded. Her voice cracked at the word happened. If he heard, he didn't show it. But after a moment, he finally turned to look at her.

"Here?"

She clenched her fists. Knuckles white. "Don't do that. No riddles. I need to know."

He almost snarled. He sighed instead. "You think I watch the dark for you?" He asked, and his words didn't match her anger. He leapt down from the perch he was resting on, coiled himself into a low spot on the floor and lay. "Child, I watch because I remember what you're not strong enough to carry on your own. You're trying to understand why. Not where. Not how. But why. And I can't give you that answer. It's not mine."

She placed the nametag back inside, then stopped; beneath a corner of loose paper, her fingers had brushed against something soft, fabric.

A sock. Too small to be hers.

Her fingers rested there. The texture carried something. She didn't reach for it. But she held still longer than she meant. Then, gently, she pulled back her hand and closed the lid. It didn't hurt. Just... not ready.

A profound, soul-deep exhaustion came over her. The urge to coil up like Sentinel. Perhaps she'd stay there and let the ash and debris coat her until some other anomaly found her bones among the wreckage.

Instead, she stood. Her knee popped. A reminder, maybe. She turned away from the box, back into the *corridor...* hallway. She leaned against the wall and pressed her forehead into the cold, gritty surface, and closed her eyes. Maybe, she didn't want answers anymore. Maybe, she just wanted the noise to stop. She reached her arm out and flicked off the light.

In the darkness, she was not alone. The outline of Sentinel's form remained, watching from a low spot on the floor, golden eyes remaining within the shadows.

Chapter 8

THE CITY SHIMMERED BEYOND the window, neon signs casting rhythmic flashes of color onto the darkened glass as night passed. The quiet inside felt like it was waiting.

She had decided to move the couch first. Her hands pressed even before she had decided where it would go. She braced herself and pushed; the couch caught on something, a stray book. Her foot slipped slightly. She muttered a curse, sharp enough to startle the quiet that settled in the corners. The unanswered wouldn't have flinched at the utterance. He'd walk through the hall of echoes, shutting out all sound.

The hall didn't welcome him. It swallowed. Upon the walls were data streams. Inscriptions crawling and moving in real time. He had begun to notice small details, though. Things that he'd normally smooth over. The sound of his footsteps softly aligning with the echoes of boot-heel clicks of forgotten agents. For the first time, he wasn't certain that he wasn't walking alone. He was wading through every moment that had come before this. A chill ran through him. Like he was mirroring the dead.

She pushed the couch again. A longer shove. The fabric groaned against the hardwood as she angled it toward the window; off-center, crooked, close enough. Her imaginary antagonist didn't even help. The nerve.

Next, the bookshelf. Books were pulled down, stacked, rearranged. Her fingers traced worn spines, familiar textures exhuming barely remembered pages. Her finger sliding along the spine sounded like the whisper of a cloak. The thud of a stacked book was the clunk of a gear locking into place as a verdict was read. Some books she hadn't visited in years, others she had meant to visit but never did. She placed the ones that mattered at eye level. The ones that still belonged.

Penelope used to say the middle shelf was for books you'd fight someone about. She'd rearranged Sable's collection once, by revenge potential.

Sable had pretended to be furious. But she hadn't moved a single one back, at least for a week or two. After that, the lack of cohesion was grating.

She found a dog-eared poetry collection, one Penelope had insisted on lending her in college. "To make you less insufferably practical," she'd said, scrawled on the inside cover. The note was in black ink, and next to it, a recipe. It was titled with the words *Rizogalo, microwave sacrilege version* in the margin, and a smiley face beside it.

She remembered Penelope laughing, explaining it was a crime against her ancestors. Something about her *yiayia*, a quiet kitchen, and a look of tectonic sadness. Sable hadn't really grasped the story then, only what it gave her. She had been seen. And she had been handed a tool.

"I'm not giving you a taste of my heritage," Penelope had said, tapping the Tupperware. "I'm giving you something to help you survive organic chemistry."

Sable hadn't laughed then. She had been too tired, too disconnected.

She laughed now. Here, in the quiet of her rearranged living room. A real laugh. The sound startled her, then she laughed again, at the memory, at the absurdity, at the impossible, practical shape of that love. She kept the book out.

Between the pages, a photograph slipped free. High school. Penelope's arm slung around her shoulder. Sable was soft-eyed, eyeliner smudged. No one commented. No one needed to.

The moving box from the other day was still in the corner near the closet. She regarded it before settling down beside it, and a tremor passed through her.

She slid it closer, and it was lighter than she expected. She reached inside and pulled out a leather-bound planner, creased and worn. She already knew what it was before she saw it, but that didn't make the weight of it any less. She almost dropped it. Almost put it back before opening it. The spine cracked, dry and barely audible. Her old handwriting filled the pages, structured, careful, a life once measured in tasks and expectations.

She flipped through the dates, the notes. Each entry was precise, meticulous. Each stroke a glyph upon a mirrored wall. Doctors appointments, deadlines, things that had once defined her days. Her eyes snagged on an alteration, an appointment scratched out. The ink seemed almost fragile, each stroke making her recall the ache of something she couldn't touch. She found something else instead. Her words so casually replaced at work, a choice taken from her. Something altered. She remembered the feeling. Like forgetting, but that was the wrong way to describe it. It was theft. Revision. The handwriting was hers, but it belonged to someone else.

Absently, she reached for her own jaw. For the scar she didn't actually have.

The unanswered passed alcoves that lined the passage, each a window or perhaps a wound. Inside them were moments of erasure frozen in motion. A mouth mid-sentence, the words fading. A face dissolving like smoke, only the eyes remaining.

He stopped at one; he shouldn't have. A figure stood before a glyph-covered wall, arms spread in defiance. It was dim, degraded. Something pulsed against the glass. Resistance maybe, or grief, and an emotion caught mid-formation. He turned away.

She closed the planner, sat it back into the box. *Be brave.* She reached further.

Her eyes were drawn to the small fabric, and she almost grasped it. A blink, and she shifted it aside instead. At the very bottom, a cool, smooth surface met her fingertips. She grasped, lifted it.

A brass sundial.

The sight of it unlocked something. A single orphan command. *Remember.*

It executed, ran through an internal loop. The end of the thread didn't tie anything together. It simply looped back onto itself, then grafted to something within her. And within the unanswered.

A feeling. She didn't recoil from it. In the hall of echoes, neither did he. The space around the unanswered emptied further. A performance before an absent audience. He grieved for what was missing, and for not noticing it before. He placed a hand against his chest and found no physical trauma. But something had rooted there.

The sundial caught the light from the campfire-bulb as she turned it. It glinted, reflecting into her eye. There was warmth there that didn't belong to her function. Or his. She remembered a choice. Not its shape. Not its context. Only the feeling of standing motionless while something greater demanded she move.

The weight of the sundial reminded her of something, but it was somehow heavier than she expected. It shouldn't have been this substantial. It shouldn't have been there at all. Her thumb ran over the ridges, the worn etchings along the surface, something meant to mark time, though it no longer served its function. There was no gnomon, no shadow to measure. It could only hold the place where time should be.

She had kept it. Just... set aside. She placed it on the bookshelf and stepped back. Like it was meant to return, but only when the forgetting grew too heavy.

The shoe box was still there. Still at the top of the closet. She pulled her eyes away from it. And that's when she saw something she had completely forgotten. In the back of the closet, another object. A canvas, tucked away. She slid it out, lifted it, turned it over, and there it was. An unfinished painting. A memory rose with it.

Colors implied more than shown, streaks of pigment layered in bold strokes, movement frozen in gesture. She remembered starting it, but not why she had stopped. Her fingertips grazed the dried paint, the textured ridges evoking echoes of unresolved thoughts, unchanged by time. She left it unfinished. She liked it better that way.

She leaned the canvas against the wall, where it could be seen. For a second, she almost turned it around, to hide it. But she didn't.

She lowered herself to the floor and sat cross-legged before the canvas. She touched it with her fingers. Let it stay A choice. She let it exist, as it was. Not as it needed to be.

Within the streaks of paint, he stood. The walls around the unanswered no longer mirrored him perfectly. Cached data, perhaps. One showed his back turned. Another, his jacket torn. One briefly showed the scar on his jawline as an open wound. And one, the most unsettling, mirrored him perfectly until it turned away, a blink before he did.

His eyes weren't turned toward the swirling colors, though. They watched her.

She shifted, turned. Palms pressed against the floor, cool.

She remembered being eleven, sitting cross-legged on the garage floor while Penelope mixed tempera paint with dish soap to make it glossy.

"You're supposed to use mediums for that," Sable had muttered, reading from a borrowed library book.

Penelope had grinned, hands covered in violet and green. "Rules are how other people forget how to remember."

Sable had never forgotten that. Even now, the unfinished painting didn't feel like failure. Just a decision held in stasis.

She stood, and turned toward the bookshelf, where the sundial remained. She almost moved it. Almost placed it back in the box. But the sight of it made her hesitate. It didn't belong, yet it didn't intrude. Her fingers hovered above it, then settled. It stayed. A breath. The space was no longer waiting. It was taking shape.

Sable stood in the center of the room, surrounded by the small changes she had made. The bookshelf, the couch, the unfinished painting, the sundial still broken, but on full display. She pivoted, her gaze falling to her phone on the counter. Her hand lifted it, fingers hovering over August's name.

Then, she typed. *Come over.*

She deleted it, backspacing all the way to *C.* Her fingers stopped.

The space around her shifted. And within that shift, something formed within her. The idea of keeping this space entirely to herself caused her shoulders to grow heavy. Too heavy.

She felt Penelope's arm on her her shoulder, nudging her toward a campfire surrounded by strangers at summer camp, whispering, *Be unbearable for five minutes. That's all it takes.*

An image of the unanswered. The hesitation he'd have standing before the archive. The place where he'd receive the next anomaly to erase. The place where he would also be erased. The cycle looping back. She thought of the orphan command. *Remember.* He turned away from it. Losing this... Losing what he was becoming... that was too much.

She retyped the words, then hit send before she could change her mind. She sat the phone down again; the screen glowed a moment longer. Then, she turned back to the moving box, lifted it, and eased it back onto the top shelf. Her fingers brushed against the shoebox as she did. Dusty, still sealed. She left it.

Part Two

Chapter 9

THE WORLD WAS WAKING. A block away, a construction site had begun excavating. The sound settled into the rough surfaces of the apartment, grasping for handholds.

Her space was bristling with intrusion. Not unkind, but present; subtle displacements and realignments that arrived without declaration. She cataloged them. A second toothbrush resting beside hers on the sink. A jacket, not hers, slung over a chair. A book, not hers, on the nightstand, left open to a dog eared page.

Sable stood in the kitchen, fingers warming themselves on her mug. She took a sip, letting the heat settle. She was not alone. August moved easily through the apartment, comfortably, like he belonged. His scent of cedar and old paper clung to the fabric of the apartment in places she hadn't invited it into.

He made coffee without asking where things were. His movements were smooth. He didn't hesitate. She did.

He sat his glass down, in no particular place. Just wherever his hand happened to land. He tapped it once and walked away. It was casual, unthinking, jarring. It rested where hers used to be. It was easy, effortless. This was what she wanted.

She expected contentment, yet a familiar coil of tension stirred within. A shift beneath the surface, a shadow stretching longer than anticipated.

She watched him load the dishwasher, the sharp clang of ceramic. Different from how she did it, different from how she had always done it. When had this became his space, too? His presence had remapped the apartment, filling spaces she never thought of as empty.

She anchored her fingers to the counter top, seeking the same handhold that the construction noise had found. It didn't want to share. She let the feeling remain, trusting that unfamiliar rhythms take time to settle.

Then she turned, moving toward the chair where her own coat rested. Her hand reached for it without thinking. She expected to feel comfort. Relief. She found neither.

She left the coat.

A golden haze suffused the apartment as afternoon arrived. Anticipation hung in the room, the kind that came before rupture. Tectonic plates that haven't budged in years.

Sable stood before a blank canvas, her fingers brushing the wooden easel as she steadied it. The old painting rested against the wall nearby, unfinished but present, a version of herself she never quite abandoned. But not yet ready to return.

She lifted a brush. Held it there, letting it settle. A hesitation. It felt different than it should. But the shape of it was familiar, the balance instinctive, as if it had never left her hand. Then she moved, a stroke. Then another. They were the first in years.

Her shoulders eased. The rhythm of paint against canvas settled something deep inside her. A part that had waited, wordless. She let herself drift into it, shielded by something unseen. Only motion remained.

August leaned against the doorway, arms crossed, watching. He waited, and so did she. For the interruption she knew would come. He tapped the side of his coffee mug. Three beats and a pause. A rhythm she had never questioned until it echoed against the silence she had chosen.

"I missed this part of you," he finally said.

The words landed softly, meant as encouragement. She recoiled, repeating it internally. 'This part of me.'

As if that's all it was. As if she was retracing steps. As if this was about returning to something lost, rather than becoming something new. Her fingers tightened around the brush. The floor was cold below her bare feet. She recalibrated her posture to match.

"Is that what you think this is?" She didn't mean for it to sound sharp. But it landed that way.

He blinked. "I just meant... Sorry. I didn't mean it like that."

She nodded. Said nothing.

Her grip on the brush loosened slightly. A choice. She stared at the canvas, searching. All she could see was what *he* thought it meant.

She tightened her grip again and then continued painting. But the rhythm had shifted, more harsh.

She wasn't just painting shapes; she was painting an argument. On one side, she worked with soft, warm, layered colors. She let them bleed and merge. Mechanical gears blurred together, creating a form that was uncertain, hazy, but full of depth. A figure not made from memory, but grown wild through it. Despite it. Its heart was a glowing ember of orange and red.

Then, on the other side, she brought in the lines. Threads from the veil. Cold and precise. She used the hard edge of her palette knife to carve lines of white and blue. Stark and clinical. They didn't blend. They severed. Hexagons formed a pattern. The Edict was born out of a collective scream. Structure emerging from disorder. Indifference coiled around a fear so controlled it had forgotten itself.

Later, the apartment felt subdued, a solitary reading lamp stretching elongated shadows across the floor. A rougher texture of quiet had seeped through the walls; less stillness than strain. The space looked the same, but it felt skewed.

Sable was curled into a corner of the couch. Her corner. An old frayed blanket draped across her shoulders. It was one from college, the pattern welcome. She wasn't reading or watching anything. Just sitting. The internal static had settled, replaced by the good kind of tired.

August sat at the other end. A reading lamp by his side. A book on civil engineering. She almost reminded him he's off the clock. But she enjoyed the crisp rustle of the pages as they turned.

A signal registered. Not from him, not even for him, really. From within. She shifted, the blanket whispering against the cushions. She slid closer, rested her head on his shoulder, testing the shape of something stirring.

Her cheek pressed against the familiar. His sweater brushed against her lips, tickled her nose. She grabbed a handful of it into her grip. Closed her fingers around it. She could smell lingering coffee from hours ago. He didn't tense. Didn't kiss her or put his own arm around her. He just... let her stay there. After a moment, his head tilted slightly, resting against hers.

Her eyes closed. It felt good to let go of something. No scanning the room. No bracing. Just... resting. Something warm. Something deliberate.

It got late. Evening routine commenced. Brush teeth, take medication, pajamas, glass of water.

Sable stood near the kitchen counter, fingers tracing the rim of her glass. The cool surface pressed into her skin, but her mind drifted elsewhere. The painting stared back at her, and with it, the words August spoke. Missing this part of her. Over her shoulder, August moved easily through the space. He fit.

She suddenly started wondering what the apartment would feel like tomorrow. Without him in it. When the warmth had faded, and only her stillness remained. Something began to build.

An idea surfaced. She almost asked if he wanted an extra pillow. Almost said something small, something easy. She almost said she needed space. Almost said nothing. But instead, something else emerged.

"What if... What if you moved in?" She could hear her heart beating in her ears. It was spontaneous, raw, and unexpected, shaped more by impulse than certainty. The words spilled from her mouth before she could stop them. Before she could consider whether she wanted to. Like stepping off a ledge and realizing too late that the ground wasn't where it should be. August blinked, then grinned.

"You sure?"

Was she? She had to be. She had no illusions about whether she was truly ready. Only, she didn't want to be alone in the aftermath of today. She would become ready. It would take time.

She nodded and a space opened inside her. It waited to feel some sort of certainty, maybe relief. But nothing settled.

"Of course." It was automatic.

August nodded back. Simple. "Okay."

A breath left her, tethering the words spoken with the feeling left unresolved. It slipped past, then was gone. He walked away, and the quiet stayed, lodging deeper within her than it should have.

The city hummed beyond the window, its distant noise pressing against the walls. Inside, time stretched itself thin, as if waiting for her to give it meaning. Sable lay awake. She twisted beneath the sheets, but no position felt right.

Beside her, August slept. Untroubled. The bed held the shape of his body like it had never held hers. She should have felt comfort. Instead, she felt elsewhere.

For a second, she almost turned toward him. Her fingers twitched. A fraction of a movement. She almost reached out. But the movement dissolved before she could commit. She stared at the ceiling and the mattress pressed upward against her back.

And she did not sleep.

Dawn's delicate fingers stretched through the blinds. Pale bands of light across the floor, a herald of the approaching day. Only, it didn't reach her.

Sable sat at the kitchen table, a cup of coffee in front of her. She hadn't taken a sip in a long time. The surface was smooth, unbroken. Her fingers pressed into the tabletop.

His jacket was still on her chair. It didn't mean anything, she told herself. But she saw it. She closed her eyes. It was supposed to help. It didn't. It felt like standing at the edge of an unremarkable chasm, waiting for something to fall but unable to let go of what she held.

The light from outside traced along the walls. Nothing moved. The coffee was still warm. She let it cool.

Chapter 10

THE APARTMENT ACCEPTED MORNING'S arrival without protest. The hum of traffic beyond the window, the sharp clink of a mug set down on the counter. The remnants of sleep pressed at the edges of her awareness. Sable moved through the motions. Reach. Lift. Coffee to lips. A rhythm practiced into muscle. She turned and reached for her coat.

Nothing. The chair was bare. It was such a small thing. A detail that shouldn't have mattered, and did. A tremble started in her knees and continued upward.

"I got you something." August's voice carried across the room, light, easy. He stood near the couch, holding a neatly folded coat. She turned to face him. The silence stretched a second too long.

"I thought it might be time for something new." His voice was warm. Encouraging. Certain.

She stepped forward, because she was supposed to. She took the coat; it felt like a script. The coat was expensive in a way she would never have chosen for herself. Her fingers skimmed along the seam, tracing what was absent, what was no longer there.

The Edict issued its decree. Not a command. A declaration. "You do not belong."

She felt the unraveling. She raged against it, even as her cloak began to fray and twist around her. Even as the veil pressed down.

"Thank you." The words were automatic. "Oh, I love the color."

August was pleased. Everything was right, for him. She put the coat on, let him see it on her. It fit. August turned away, smiling. He adjusted a chair, flipped through a book, filled a glass with practiced ease. He didn't notice the way she stood. Sable kept her hands in her pockets, fingers pressing into the lining. The fabric was smooth under her fingers. But blank. A thing newly bought, not yet shaped by presence. The coat should have been reassuring. It wasn't.

"I was thinking we could go somewhere later. Get out for a bit." August's voice was casual, at ease. He didn't look up at first, assuming the answer would come easily, naturally. But it didn't. The pause dragged, thin and uneven. She should have answered. She should have said something.

It wasn't that she was losing focus. She was slipping. Horribly. She had an idea that her skin was becoming porous. Like liquid was filling the spaces between cells.

The boundary between her and *not her* thinned, until it was irrelevant.

Beneath the chaos, the noise of it all, one thought remained. A physical sensation. Something she held onto even if she couldn't actually feel it now. She could force herself to remember it. Its rough texture. The loose thread at the hem. She counted.

One. Two. Three.

August glanced over, waiting. Sable blinked, surfaced. Her throat tightened, the words reluctant, resisting. When she finally spoke, her voice cracked.

"Maybe," she answered.

August looked satisfied. He didn't see the way she pulled in air too quickly, the way her shoulders tightened under the coat as if it had settled wrong. She pressed her hands deeper into the pockets. Her body held still, as if that could deny what trembled within her.

Evening stretched over the apartment, drawing shadows that blurred the room's edges. August glided through the kitchen, washing his hands, drying them on a towel. It sounded like the natural sounds of home. Water running, the sharp clang of dishes.

Sable perched on the bed, brushing her hair. The new coat loomed beside her. Her fingers skittered without rhythm or anchor along the fabric. It was too sleek, unmarked by time or use. The movements were small, restless, as if searching for the roughness, the frayed edges that should have been there but weren't. It wasn't that she longed for the coat's fray; she longed for the texture of a hand that had once found hers through it.

August stepped beside her, resting a warm hand on her shoulder. It didn't comfort. He leaned in, pressing a kiss to her hair like an afterthought. His gaze caught on the coat beside her and he smiled, mistaking silence for agreement. "I always felt bad when you wore that thing in the rain." Her hand stopped. A pause. Almost nothing.

He shifted, barely perceptible. But then, he kept moving. His voice was light, reassuring. "This one's warmer," he said. "You deserve something nice." His words didn't waver. He was certain. The gesture, to him, felt right.

This was a kindness. So why did she feel the cage door shut? She should have been grateful. August left the room and moved to the couch, reaching for the remote, settling in. The moment was already gone for him. But she was sitting in it.

Four. Five. S-s... Six.

It wasn't working. Then through the static, a sound. It rose above the shriek of the grinding gears of the Edict above her and the hum of the veil enveloping her.

A low rumble. Ancient. Heavy as bedrock. A dark shadow before her. Sentinel. A sound tore from his throat. It couldn't have been categorized as a word spoken, but a sound clawed from the depths of his being. A ragged, desperate expulsion of air that took the shape of her name.

"Sable!"

He tugged at her cloak, but it came apart in shreds between his teeth. He was trying to get her back on her feet. She looked down, and she had no feet to stand on. There hadn't even been the sensation of falling. Or perhaps she had been falling for so long, she hadn't noticed the ground arrive below her. She looked up into his eyes and saw past the immutable fire of the guardian. The golden slits reflected back something that made her want to weep.

He hadn't done this for her. He had done this to survive her.

The warmth of the room didn't reach her limbs, it lingered in the corners instead. The hum of the television, the clink of a glass set down, it all moved forward without her.

Sable stood near the door. A blink and her shoes were already on. When had she decided to move? The floor felt distant beneath her steps, disconnected, as if she were only an observer to her own movement. The door handle was cool under her fingers, strange. Had she never touched it before? She left the new coat on the bed.

As she crossed the threshold, August's voice drifted from the couch, half-distracted. "Where are you going?"

She didn't turn. "Just getting some air." she said.

He waited. Then a hum of acknowledgment. "You won't be out long, right?"

She stepped outside.

The chill gripped her. No hesitation. It settled into the space where warmth should have been. The cold bit at her skin, threading through her hair, slipping beneath the collar of her sweater, winding through the marrow of her bones.

She felt the words on her tongue. Tried to say them. *I deserve to be here. I don't deserve to be erased.* But no sound emerged. The veil ripped away her voice. If it carried, it was only an echo. A whisper. Her mythic form vanished, leaving behind only ash upon stone.

She exhaled, slow, watching her breath ghost into the night. The lights from passing cars smeared at the edges. Her coat was gone; the cold took its place.

It found a home and she let it remain. A cold she would not shake.

Chapter 11

MORNING. THE DAY'S MUTED rhythm began. Only, she didn't move with it. The heater exhaled and fell silent, its warmth receding into corners she didn't occupy. Outside, the city hummed. A backdrop of engines, footsteps, voices. They were separate from her, distant like sound behind glass.

August sat a mug in front of her. Steam lifted, winding upward, like thinning tendrils that vanished before reaching her face. The space between warmth and contact was insurmountable. But still, she extended her hand to the mug.

An offering. In her mind, Sentinel accepted, resting his paw on the unanswered's hand. Static and fur without ceremony. It was expected. An acknowledgement of one ruin upon another. Sentinel had never been allowed to refuse kindness like this. And still, it was a test. Sentinel needed to know if the unanswered's skin still buzzed like the Edict. It felt human enough to be tolerable.

The chair held her shape, but she hovered inside it; as if it belonged to someone else. She returned her hands to her lap, uncommitted. Two separate things.

"The Edict will look again," Sentinel rumbled. "It has to ensure the severance was clean," His voice was the sound of a tomb door scraping across dusty stone. "It's pointless to stay."

The unanswered's gaze remained on the empty space. On the echo of her. "If I had acted sooner," he said. "Maybe. Maybe, the outcome would be different. There was a moment. You didn't see it. My fingers reached for the sword, but I stayed. I could have done something. But I didn't. My feet wouldn't move."

Sentinel snarled. "Mine did. And the thread snapped all the same." Silence stretched between them. The veil was moving closer. "Stop acting like this is the first time you lost her. Get up."

Across the room, August with his rhythmic ease. The muted shuffle of his steps. Spoon and ceramic. The tap of his phone against the counter. He glanced over. "You've got a full day?"

She waited. Her fingers pressed into her lap, as if grounding herself in the motion.

"Yeah." Nothing more. The answer felt foreign in her mouth. She drank her coffee while it was still too hot. She might not otherwise.

The train rumbled beneath her, steady and impersonal. Movement flowed, shoulders brushing past, damp umbrellas dripping onto the floor, the sour scent of wet fabric and moss rising in waves. Announcements crackled, windows blurred with rain, and the hum of fluorescent lights wove through it all. She remained, a fixed point in motion.

Sentinel was prowling somewhere nearby, and the unanswered felt more than just unease. He had tried to erase her. The anomaly. Sable. And though he failed, she was gone now. He didn't expect forgiveness.

A small, firm pressure against her thigh startled her from her stillness; a child, no older than five, had steadied himself with a hand on her leg. His fingers pressed into the fabric of her pants. Her muscles flinched.

He looked up at her, a wide grin, as if he had the most amazing story to tell her. Then his expression changed. The grin fell and his eyes widened. He pulled his hand away, as if burned. Without a word, he scurried back to his mother and buried his face in her coat.

He slipped away, the specter of his fingers still imprinted on her leg and the look in his eyes lingered. She recognized that look. She had seen it all her life,

At work, she stepped through the motions. The badge swipe. The hallway. The shared research suite. In the breakroom, the scent of over-brewed coffee clung to the

walls. Fluorescent lights signaled warnings that nobody heeded, washing every surface in the same indifferent pallor. Fogged windows let in a dim light that felt more like absence than day. Each space arrived without intention, then faded. Everything blended.

Matthew passed, an easy nod. "Morning, Katherine." And nothing more.

Sable blinked. She didn't correct him. The name drifted down, like dust settling on something long forgotten.

Sentinel and the unanswered walked through the hall of echoes. Past the same alcoves as before. A profound wrongness settled over them. The frayed and worn edges of the Loom were beginning to mend. Too fast. It looked like healing, but it was only a shallow mimicry of it. It all looked like a freshly polished scar. The blackened glass walls gleamed. It was running diagnostics, searching for the last remnants of corruption. Sentinel was not safe here.

At her desk, her pen hovered. The page waited, the text looking back up at her, asking a question: *What tools are you using?*

She wrote it. *Katherine.* The name formed without effort. It didn't bother her that much. Not anymore. It was easier not to fight.

The elevator hummed. The hallway stretched ahead, unchanged. Carpet worn thin at the corners. Light diffused through frosted panels. It tasted bland on her tongue. Where had the day gone? There was no memory of it. Only this bland, empty space between morning and now.

Evening came. She stepped into the bedroom. The scent of laundered cotton and rain-soaked branches. A narrow band of light on the hallway floor halted before the mirror. Dust drifted in the beam, suspended, as if it had forgotten how to move.

Sentinel looked up at his companion through the uneven light. The unanswered held himself rigidly still. It made the fur on his spine rise. It didn't feel like he was walking through a gallery. It felt like a queue. A waiting room disguised as a museum. The unanswered walked like a man trying to mimic a statue, even if that statue was a fucking lie.

August was in the other room, the television a low murmur. She sat on the edge of the bed, the mattress dipping slightly. Beside her, where she'd tossed it that morning, was the new coat.

The texture of the day's resentment surfaced. This object, this monument to how little he understood what she actually needed. Her gaze caught on the seam of the shoulder, a perfectly straight, unflinching line of thread. She thought it might run off the coat and out the door. And a different thought pushed through.

August didn't do things impulsively. Every choice he made was a quiet calculation. The world was a spreadsheet, and each moment a cell within it. She let the image form. Him, in a department store. The soft, impersonal music, the scent of leather and wool. He wouldn't have been looking at the color. He would have been running the fabric between his thumb and forefinger, assessing its weave. He would have checked the tag for its material blend, judged its durability against a bad forecast. He would have compared three others, weighing the variables of function and longevity.

He wouldn't have been thinking, *This is beautiful.* He would have been thinking, *This is a good system. This will keep her safe.*

The thought didn't bring comfort. It brought something else. Something more complicated than anger. Draped across the bed was a solution to her problems. A fortress against the cold, built with the only tools he had. The coat wasn't a criticism of her. It was a perfect portrait of *him.* The thought occurred to her, that the unanswered was not the Edict's blade. He was its acolyte. A priest to a god of emptiness. And that his scar wasn't a battle wound, but a seal of his office.

The texture of the coat didn't ease. Now it had company. Now it had a history. A shared space that crowded the bad texture. She didn't touch the coat. She just looked at it for a long time, its perfect, unyielding shape was stark in the dimming light. She turned away.

The mirror waited, half-shadowed, its edge caught in the last reach of hallway light stretching across the glass. She slowed. Her breath stumbled, as if her body knew what her mind wouldn't say. There she was. But it felt like she was looking at a photograph. Something distant. Removed.

Her fingers twitched, as if she might reach out and touch the glass. The thought was there, enough to be real, not enough to act upon. Her balance wavered. Her toes pressed into the floor, but she didn't quite claim the sensation.

It was easier not to. Less costly. Her breath settled. Nothing shifted. Instead, a quiet dread within her began to grow roots. Maybe if she could understand *why*, it might help. She looked deeper into the mirror. Past her own reflection, if it was really hers.

"I think I heard my own scar," the unanswered said. Sentinel had withdrawn into the shadows. He was walking the perimeter, but out of sight. His claws tapped on the tile floor. Click. Click. Click. "What are you doing?" the unanswered asked.

"I'm introducing a flaw," he said, coldly. "Now, tell me what you heard."

"My function..." he choked, the word a blasphemy on his tongue. "It wasn't to unmake. It was to... reset. To clean up the mess after it was done."

The alcoves around them looked perfect. Immaculate. But now, they understood the terrible nature of that perfection. The true role. He was the one sent in after the sacrifice was complete. To wash the altar, to close the book.

To keep the world legible. And worse, to keep him legible to himself, at the cost of everything.

"I just realized something," the panther said from somewhere in the darkened chamber. His voice came as an exhausted growl. "I suppose I'm the next name to be erased."

She turned away from the mirror without another look back, but a part of her wondered what she had left behind there. There was no sorrow in her. No comfort either. Only the image, still there, still watching. Still not quite hers.

Chapter 12

THE MORNING HELD, BUT time had come undone. The sheets were tangled around her legs, caught in restless movements she didn't remember. The ceiling felt closer.

It felt strange to wake this slowly, her awareness drifting upward through a fog, guided only by the faintest threads of habit. She rose mechanically, each movement unfolding without conscious intent. The sheets pressed against her skin, anchoring her in an unfinished embrace. A car hummed past outside, the sound rising and fading.

A dread coiled just under her ribs. Like the Edict's mechanical eye had fixed upon her. A dream, maybe.

The unanswered stood within the hush of the archive. He was no longer a stranger to what it held. He listened. And from its depths, he heard the sound of threads thrumming. Four of them, each note stinging against his eardrums.

Cold greeted her beyond the blankets, detached and impersonal. The floor beneath her feet sent a sharp, indifferent chill through her bones. The morning didn't require her presence to unfold.

The bitter scent of coffee drifted, inviting. August sat a mug beside her. Her body never registered it. The steam curled upward, fragile, already unraveling.

Thread one. The anomaly's smile. Small, trusting. It landed like a warmth spreading across the unanswered's chest. So intense it almost burned. Her gaze fixed on his face, not on the controls he was adjusting.

She had left her keys on the counter. They didn't feel like hers at first. She looked too long before finally reaching for them, mapping out each step. It should have been automatic. Routine had moved her forward and she was already exhausted by the level of intention the day was requiring of her. She picked up the mug and took it with her.

The warmth of coffee blended into the muted glow of office lights, seamless. Like fog changing shape. The mug in her hand had cooled. She drank it anyway.

Thread two. The unanswered's own fingers. Tap. Tap. Tap. The lie coiled in his gut. A small price. A necessary mercy to shield her. His love was a beacon. He would dim it, for their own good.

She forgot a meeting, her mind skimming over its absence, barely noting the lapse before continuing. The day pressed forward. She moved through it, but had difficulty holding onto it. Tasks blurred together; query responses drafted, lab values transcribed, screening logs updated, none of them staying long enough to register. By the time she blinked, an hour was gone. And then, the day had already slipped away.

The office had been filled with movement that felt unnatural. Conversations overlapped, voices droning into a hostile texture. Someone laughed near the coffee machine. The printer clicked and whirred, spitting out pages. Phones rang. Keyboards clattered. The fluorescent lights cast everything in the same muted glow. Every surface was an abrasion waiting for a target.

Thread three. The low hum in the air. A sudden drop in temperature, hollowing in the unanswered's gut. Like he had just fallen from a high place. The veil twisted, constricting tighter. The Edict's attention turned, a vast and indifferent eye honing in on the deviation. Gears shifted into place.

Sable sat at her desk, staring at the open visit summary. The fields blurred, collapsed, reformed strangely. She blinked, but they didn't sharpen. She heard a voice at the edge of her awareness, pulling her back. Matthew stood beside her, pointing to a discrepancy in the dosing log. Her fingers hovered over the keyboard.

She held the script in her hands. The formula of response, rehearsed day in and day out. Embarrassment should have come. A need to correct the error. Neither did. She forced a response.

"Oh. Sorry." The words felt empty. Matthew nodded, moved on. The thought of the mistake stretched, then disappeared beneath everything else.

Thread four. The severing. The unanswered couldn't see anything, but he could feel it. A name being scraped from his own mind. Not just hers. And in the hollow space it left, a new designation was branded. The unanswered. A function. A mask that rendered her invisible by erasing the one who saw her most clearly.

Time folded. The moment passed. Her surroundings melted from one space to the next. She didn't even remember the journey home.

August spoke to her. His fingers traced the rim of his glass before he exhaled louder than he likely intended. His gaze flicked toward her, searching without meeting her eyes. The hush lasted longer than it should have. His words skimmed over, never quite landing. He exhaled once, shifted uncomfortably in his chair, fingers tightening briefly around his glass. He was gathering the courage to try again. Only he didn't.

She gave a nod, and nothing more. The choice was made somewhere else. The phone's vibration intruded, sharply breaking a moment neither of them had willingly acknowledged.

"They took my name, and I didn't even fight. I thanked them for the quiet." The unanswered choked on the word. "I was the blade and the mask. But... I was trying to protect her."

Sentinel cocked his head. "Oh, so she was part of this too then? She... asked you? Invited you?" His eyes narrowed, golden slits like daggers. "You made a choice for her. There is a difference."

August's voice kept moving through the space between them, trying to close the distance. Words passed, light but searching. He was waiting, for a signal maybe. She didn't give it to him. Eventually, he stopped trying.

The sound of silverware against porcelain, the distant hum of traffic outside. The world continued. Voices moved around her, easy, familiar, sounds she once joined without thinking. Now, she listened and said nothing. The words drifted past, carrying with them the cadence of a routine she no longer stepped into.

Sentinel had withdrawn into the shadows. Only his eyes were visible. Fixed and haunting. A predator stalking its prey. "Why don't you ask the Edict? Go look for a protocol to justify your grief, unanswered."

"Don't," he replied. It's all he could manage.

"Don't?" Sentinel continued moving forward. Head low. Muscles tensing. "Don't what, unanswered? Don't you have a long overdue deviation log to file? Some function to carry out? A beast to kill?"

The unanswered put a hand in front of him. "Don't... don't call me that. That's not who I am. That's not my name, or my title."

Later at work, someone made a joke. Natural, unforced laughter rose around her. The familiar rhythm, the pause where she would have joined in. Her absence didn't interrupt the flow. No one noticed. The world moved. People spoke. Voices filled the space.

She was present in the room, but she was no longer part of it. Time slipped past her, unspooling. Day dissolved into night, and night into day.

Shadows lengthened across the apartment. The heater hummed. Outside, streetlights flickered on, casting lines of light along the floor. Warmth reached her skin, but the space felt distant, like a room she hadn't stayed in long enough to claim.

Something must have drawn her eyes there. It wasn't conscious. Her eyes were just... lingering there. She could have been staring at anything. Only, she wasn't. She was looking at the sundial.

The unanswered shifted his gaze to the pedestal rising from the floor. To the artifact that rested on it. The sound of the pedestal was rough, stone against stone. Two tectonic plates aligning. "She held something once," he said. "Something that mattered."

She felt a tear threaten to emerge. She buried it. August stood by the counter, scrolling through his phone. He spoke absently without looking up. "I made a reservation for Friday. Thought it'd be nice." His tone was light, casual, as if this was something they had agreed on.

Sable didn't answer right away. She let the steam curl from the tea he had left on the table, undisturbed. The surface of the liquid stilled, cooling. He glanced at her. "That okay?"

She blinked, nodded. "Yeah." She didn't ask. Deciding took more than she had.

The unanswered picked up the sundial from the pedestal. He brushed his thumb against the raised letter. Only one. The rest had been scoured away. The letter, V.

"That shouldn't be here," Sentinel said.

The unanswered ignored him. He no longer feared the panther; he didn't have the energy to. If he chose to maul him, he'd just be mauled. No sense making it a problem. He turned the sundial in his hands. Tried to remember why it was important. The blade at the top was missing. What's the point of a sundial that casts no shadow?

But then he remembered something. Kneeling beside her at the observatory. His hand over hers at the dial. And her, or someone shaped like her, looking out a window. Breath fogging on glass she couldn't open. A coat draped over a chair.

"I was once called Vesper," he finally said. "That was my name."

Everything hurt. More than usual, at least. The light, the dark, the sound, the silence. Whispers felt like scratches. Anything more might require stitches. Her own shoes felt constricting. The light in the *chamber*... living room, strobed once. A deviation in the power grid. It didn't go out. She wished it would. She looked out the window. Tried to find Sentinel. She wondered where he would be. Stalking? Hiding? Or just... uninterested.

Later, a doctor's appointment appeared on the calendar hanging on the wall. She hadn't scheduled it. Her name sat there, written in August's neat handwriting. A time. A place. A decision made for her. She stared at it, her gaze tracing the ink as if that might make it feel more like hers. It didn't. She moved on.

The coat was on the chair. It was not the old one, the texture that she once knew. It was the new one, the coat August had given her. The fabric was crisp, the folds sharp, shaped by absence. It had been there for days, its presence constant. The chair had adjusted to it, as if accustomed to it in a way it was not accustomed to her. It belonged to the chair more than she belonged to this space.

Darkness settled over the apartment. There was only the glow of her phone screen, casting pale light across the sheets. A name. *Penelope.*

The call vibrated against the nightstand, insisting. She held her breath, fingers hovering above the screen, before exhaling and swiping the notification away. The sound barely registered. A flicker of presence that never fully arrived. The screen dimmed and the room emptied as the light faded.

It began with a fracture. The formation of a faultline. The first cut had been Vesper's; the rest belonged to the Loom.

The phone vibrated again. This time, she didn't fully reach for it. Her fingers twitched, an automatic impulse to pick it up, but she stopped midway. The screen's glow lingered, a ghost touching the ceiling, an echo of what hadn't been spoken.

When it ceased, she finally reached out and flipped the phone over, face down, burying the light. She closed her eyes, pressed her fingers into the mattress, but the pressure didn't reassure her.

Chapter 13

THE OFFICE HAD GONE stale. A constant, dull presence. Burnt coffee near the breakroom, gray suits tinged with printer ink. She almost longed for the mood to become rotten just to give the office some kind of taste.

Sable sat at her desk, her fingers resting against the edge, unmoving. She opened the adverse event summary. Blood pressure spike, nausea, flagged as possibly related. But the words slid past.

It happened again. The same voice, the same pause. Matthew stopped beside her desk. "Hey, there's a data mismatch in this section again." He waited. The words reverberated against her ribs. Again.

She knew this moment. She had lived it before, more than once. It landed like a calendar notification. A breath. A blink. Nothing more. She used to dive into mistakes like these like a puzzle that needed to be solved. Now they echoed.

She lifted her eyes, her gaze hovering in that unfocused way that didn't invite more. Matthew's face became unreadable. He adjusted, like he would say more, but then moved on.

She could have fixed the mistake, but she didn't; the report stayed open. She took a sip of her coffee and recoiled. It hadn't been warm for a long time. A phone rang somewhere. When had it stopped? It must have passed the way all the other moments had. Without shape, without her involvement. She just wasn't here. She was watching the hollow spire.

The first step into the spire's influence was a fall. The air became a dense soup of whispers. A thousand conversations ending mid-word. Vesper gripped the hilt of his sword, but the metal was a riot against his skin. The spire was showing him everything. The air became a torrent of sensory data. Stress fractures spiderwebbed in the stone under his feet. The silent, screaming decay of a single thread in the veil a mile away grated at his ears. Light was a cascade of individual photons, each one a searing pinprick against his retinas. A wave of nausea rolled through him as his inner ear, bombarded by a million contrary vibrations, lost its sense of equilibrium.

It was the unfiltered source code of the world. A thousand conflicting thoughts and sensations. It was erasing him with its sheer, meaningless volume.

And through the chaos, a figure spun from haze directly in front of him. It held Sable's posture. It wore her coat... cloak. Its face was smoothed, like one of the oracles, but its voice was a perfect crystalline replica of hers. Of Sable's. "A small price," it whispered, syllables crackling. "This was to protect us."

Later, near the copy room, she heard Matthew again, his voice echoing down the hallway. Another joke, this one thinly veiled. She didn't catch all of it, only the edge of a sentence, something about spicy food. The kind of joke that always sounded like a compliment until it wasn't. Priya stiffened. Didn't stop walking. Didn't answer.

Sable intervened, the script falling aways somewhere, forgotten. "Matthew." She heard herself call to him. It was louder than she expected.

He turned, a lazy, questioning look on his face. "Hmm?"

Sable took a moment, but kept her expression neutral. She pushed her glasses up. "That joke, what was the intended outcome?" She asked it like it was a simple data point.

The question startled him. Unusual. He raised his hands. "What? It was just a joke."

"I know," Sable said, detached. Her tone was perfectly even, as if she'd just pinpointed a variable. "I'm asking about the expected result. Was the goal camaraderie? A release of tension? Improved team morale?"

She didn't accuse him; she analyzed. She held his words up to the light like a flawed piece of data. Sable glanced over at Priya. She was further now, but she had stopped. Her hands were folded across her chest. She wasn't looking at Matthew, though. She was looking at her. Priya's jaw clenched, then her eyes darted up the hall, then back to her.

Matthew's face flushed. "It's not that deep. It was just funny."

"Okay," Sable said. She held his gaze longer than he would have liked. "Thank you for clarifying."

He backed off, shaking his head. The hallway cleared.

Sable turned to Priya, reflex more than intention. A gesture meant to show solidarity, maybe. Or a signal that she'd seen it. It didn't land. Priya met her gaze, and for a second, something like disappointment flickered behind her eyes.

"Next time," Priya said. "Let me speak for myself." Priya stopped in the doorway. She turned back, measured. "I know it makes you feel better to fix things," she went on. "But I don't need you to fix me."

Then she walked away.

Sable stood motionless. The sound of the copier hummed behind her, too loud. Her hand twitched slightly at her side. She went back to her desk and began staring at a line of numbers she'd already forgotten twice. Enrollment logs. Lab values. Missing signatures. All blurring. The report hadn't fixed itself. The cursor blinked, patient and unbothered. The blank notepad was there. And a pen. A tool. Something she could use. She started to reach.

"Is now a good time?"

Her eyes didn't move from the notepad and pen.

Matthew stood beside her desk, papers in hand, face composed into a well rehearsed calm. A little too measured. Like he was being generous. Like he was pretending nothing had happened.

"You seemed a little... off, earlier."

She blinked. "I'm fine." What if she threw her cup of coffee onto him? The image of the cold brown liquid staining his pristine shirt nearly made her laugh aloud. She held it in, mostly.

He nodded, as if that answered something. "Just a small discrepancy in the Q3 compliance column. No big deal. I'll flag it for you."

He sat the papers down. Picked up her pen. He circled the error, then absently dropped the pen into his pocket.

"Let me know if you need any help." His tone was even, the kind people used when they thought they were being useful. His fingers tapped once against the edge of her desk.

They lingered there, on her desk, a little too long. Then he turned away, satisfied with himself. Maybe a little concerned, even. His footsteps faded. The report stayed open, and the cursor kept blinking. She ached for the frayed edge of her coat, but found only her bare arms. She scratched hard enough to leave red lines.

Fluorescents buzzed. Printers coughed. Somebody's chair let out a rubbery squeal. Every sound arrived peeled of distance, scraping. It was all just too loud, too close.

·"It's too much." The words came out in a whisper. Vesper's knees were buckling.

"Of course it is," Sentinel snarled, weaving through the chaos that seemed to bend around him. "It's a system. It found your greatest vulnerability and it's exploiting it." He glared. "It's what you would have done."

Vesper's face went blank. He was useless here.

Sentinel's lips peeled back from his teeth, fury rising. "Then let it drown you!" He snarled, his voice a ragged, sawblade of a sound. "Let it tear you apart. You think the veil cares about your pain? You think it will pause because you feel overwhelmed? It is a function. It will erase you without logging the event. You won't get an alcove. No sword. No scar. People will walk over the dust of your bones and not even remember that you were there. And they won't care, either."

He lowered his head. A predator's posture, crowding Vesper's space. "You are noise. You are a vulnerability. Stop trying to find a protocol for this. Find a reason to survive that isn't just a lie you tell yourself. Or die here and be quiet about it."

She slid from her chair, walked past the copy room, past the women's restroom and slipped into the single-stall restroom instead.

Click. Bolt engaged.

Tile glare, white-white walls, porcelain. A ballast hum that hid nothing. She leaned both palms on the sink, counting the eight blue and white hexagons under her right thumb while her pulse kicked along her jaw.

Faucet left... scalding. Faucet right... cold.

Five hot breaths, five cold. Skin stung.

The citrus-antiseptic soap foamed a smell strong enough to shove the burnt-coffee haze out of her head. She rubbed until bubbles grayed, then let the water run longer than needed, watching it braid away.

The mirror offered a too-bright version of her face. Her badge hung from her lanyard, tilted: *Sable*. The letters looked like they wanted to slide off the plastic. She tapped it once, tactile confirmation, then looked away because the light kept bleaching her edges.

The paper towel machine rasped, one, two, folded into silent compresses she slipped into her pants pocket like relics.

Hand-dryer roar? Too much. She left it silent.

Click. Bolt released.

The door eased open and the corridor din rushed back in, but felt manageable. Like the stall walls were still holding part of the noise for her. She walked toward her desk, fingers slightly damp, smelling of synthetic citrus. Matthew glanced up, said nothing, and the day resumed, out of sync, but still moving.

Daylight sank below the horizon, leaving the apartment dim. The curtains stirred from the vents, but the space still felt unchanged. Distant, even. The phone vibrated on the nightstand. Once. Twice. Penelope.

Sable watched it. Her hand lifted slightly, then hovered. The impulse faded before it fully formed. She didn't move. She waited. In case it vibrated again. It didn't.

A notification waited, a remnant of a conversation she wasn't ready for. She swiped it away. The evening stretched and avoided filling the space the call left behind. Her shoulders dropped. The tension didn't.

She brushed her thumb across the screen without knowing why, then sat the phone down, face first, as if that could undo the fact that it had rung at all.

Once, Penelope had told her that grief made you chronically early.

"You show up to everything ten minutes ahead," she'd said, handing Sable a watch with a cracked face, the battery removed, "because the moment you're late, they'll think you've forgotten. And you didn't."

She had worn that watch for a while.

The glow faded from the sheets. The name remained, unseen. Time slipped forward, folding. Shadows stretched, as if trying and failing to reclaim the spaces between moments.

Somewhere outside, a car door slammed. A dog barked. The world moved on.

Sable turned over. The bed compressed slightly beneath her as she settled. Her gaze avoided the window. The glass might offer a version of her that she couldn't trust. She closed her eyes, though she didn't feel tired. It was too early to sleep.

She must have got up, given up on rest, because she was sitting at the table. A half-eaten plate of food rested in front of her. She couldn't remember whether she had eaten. The apartment felt smaller than usual. The walls held in what was certain, but certainty occupied less space than it had before. The overhead light was warm but dim, halos bleeding across the kitchen counter. She could smell food, but it barely registered.

The fork was still in her hand; she didn't remember lifting it. She sat it down, now. Quietly. As if sound might shatter a thread she held in both hands.

August leaned against the counter. His fingers tapped once against the wood, then stopped. He had no right to judge her like that. He looked like he might speak. *Don't. Please don't.*

"You've been quiet lately."

She didn't answer right away. Her silence wasn't guarded, just... nothing came. She picked the fork back up, nudged a piece of food. The motion was empty.

"I don't know," she said eventually. A line that had been rehearsed in a dream. Shouted from the top of the spire.

August watched her. She didn't look back, but his gaze pressed into her. It cut between skin cells. He didn't know what to say and that pierced deeper than any question could have. Time slowed. Something flickered in his eyes, uncertainty, maybe. Concern, maybe. But he didn't press.

She sat the fork aside again. It clanged against the ceramic, reverberating through her elbow. Across her spine. The food had gone cold. She wasn't sure it had ever been warm.

The hallway light spilled a narrow glow across the bedroom floor. Sable stopped in the doorway, her hand resting on the frame. The warmth of the light brushed her skin but didn't settle. It felt borrowed, like it belonged to another night, or another world. The air was cool. The walls threatened to move closer. She caught sight of herself in the hallway mirror again. Still not her.

She tried to remember when she had changed. The glass didn't answer. It only returned her gaze, but left it unreadable. The feeling faded before it resolved. She started to turn away. But then, a glimmer. In the edge of the glass, a shape behind her. *The sundial.*

It sat on the shelf, partially hidden in shadow. Her fingers twitched. For a second, the weight of it was in her palm. She used to carry it without thinking. Now, looking at it from across the room nearly broke her. Even imagining it felt like trespass.

What if... what if I can't do this anymore? What if it was time to let go. To put the sundial away. To put on the coat. To become Katherine again.

Vesper reeled. He was at his last edges. "I can't," he whispered. He looked up and saw the panther move on through the labyrinth-like spire. He would continue on, without him. He'd really just leave him here.

Something about that filled him with rage. But, not for Sentinel. He wanted to apologize. For taking away what they had. What they once held. Only, that wouldn't have been for her. It would have been for him. Words began to form. It felt like an incantation on his lips. Not even a shred of defiance or grief was left. It was just... the only thing he had left.

"I didn't deserve to be erased," he whispered.

Her world snapped back into some semblance of focus. The thought flickered, then faded. Words almost spoken. An image brushed the edge of her thoughts, just out of reach. There were memories she didn't reach toward. She hadn't forgotten them. She couldn't. And that was the problem. She pulled the blanket over her shoulders, letting a corner drag onto the floor as she walked. The hallway light hummed behind her. She left it on. The reflection remained, unseen.

Sable stood in the threshold of the living room, surveying. The new coat stared back. Its fabric had slumped in the same shape, creased by its own weight. It just sat there, unchanged, familiar in the way absence becomes. It knew she wouldn't pick it up. That was the point. Her chest tightened, clenched around nothing. She imagined herself picking it up, tearing it into two. The sound, the rupture it might make. She almost hoped it would hurt. The coat didn't move. She wished it would.

She reached for the light switch, and as the room dimmed, shadows stretching into the corners, she turned away. And she let the shadows fold behind her. There was no sense in watching them settle.

Chapter 14

Sable lay motionless beneath the blankets. Her limbs were stiff, and her own breath disturbed the quiet. The coolness pressed through the fabric. Her body registered what her mind couldn't. The morning didn't feel new. It simply repeated. A looping thread, unstitched from one morning directly into the next. Maybe that's why she let it stretch. Maybe that's why she stayed there. She hadn't moved. The alarm rang hours ago, but she barely remembered it. Time continued, and the day passed without her stepping into it.

Light slipped through the blinds, casting lines across the ceiling. She hadn't checked the time. The phone rested face-down on the nightstand and reaching for it would require more energy than she had. A sliver of light emerged from under the edge, the only indication of life within it.

From the other room, August's presence filtered through the walls. Dishes, water, a news report. She wanted him to drop a glass. She listened for it without meaning to. He never did, of course. The sounds were far away, like they belonged to a different life. But they kept intruding on hers.

Eventually, she shifted onto her side. She wouldn't sleep, only some instinct demanded that she change something anyway. Like a different angle might solve it all. The shadows on the ceiling stretched and pulled back, marking hours she hadn't participated in. Eventually, her fingers reached for the phone. Missed calls. Messages. A summary of a meeting she hadn't attended. She scrolled without reading, then sat it down again.

It isn't that she decided to stay; she never decided to go. The thought hadn't had the chance to fully form. It only pressed at the edges of awareness. A breath. Then nothing. The refrigerator clicked on and off. It kept returning. Like ritual. She agonized over its pattern. To decipher its meaning. Was there some sort of message contained within it? Audible glyphs cast on white walls that might hold secrets the world wanted to erase.

The citadel knew. A low, accusatory thrum began to radiate from the chamber's walls. A pressure wave had begun to constrict around the third oracle's form. The inscriptions that lined the corridors wrapped around them like a cage. Each glyph a bar. Order. Precision. The rhythm of the Edict. For eons, it had been a comfort. The steady, predictable heartbeat of existence. Now, it was a metronome counting down to their own correction.

Footsteps, sharp and precise, clicked against the floor. The second oracle emerged from the shadows, their glow so pure and cold that it seemed to suck the warmth from the air around it.

"You are misaligned," the second oracle stated flatly. "Your resonance signature is... noisy. Fix it." They scanned their whole body as if to pinpoint the origin of the disturbance. "What did you touch at the faultline? What did you fail to purge?"

The first oracle approached, until now only a silent observer in this exchange. "They don't seem that off to me. It could be that they are only imitating divergence. We've seen true anomalies before. They flicker, but only a little. They've been productive thus far."

A low hum resonated across the chamber. The third oracle shifted, caught between two tectonic plates. They began to question themself. Words began to form. A defense? Against what? Which accusation was the most dangerous?

"Or perhaps the silence was the problem all along," they said. They let their voice drift, deliberately off-key. They watched the second oracle recoil from it. The first oracle seemed pleased.

Sable stood in front of the closet, her fingers on the door. She didn't know why she'd come. Only that she had. The shoebox was on the top shelf, tucked behind folded blankets. It was heavier than she remembered. Or maybe she was different now. She brought it down, then sank to the floor with it held between her fingers. Being this close to it left her hands trembling, her throat swollen.

Dust clung to the cardboard, though smeared from the day she had found the sundial in the moving box beside it. Her fingers trailed through the dust, pulling it, interrupting it. Her hand hovered over the edge of the filament tape that sealed it shut.

She stopped. Inside, a thread of something held in suspension. A sound, or memory, or weight. Some things lose their shape when you haven't looked at them in a while. Others return sharper.

She traced the line of the tape once more, then pushed the box back into the closet. She didn't have the energy to lift it back to the shelf. Just slid it barely inside the door instead.

Something had already begun to open. Something that flickered. Maybe memory, maybe refusal. Or maybe the echo of folding herself small enough to go unnoticed. She closed the door, trying to seal it shut. Behind her, the room didn't change. The citadel didn't seem to notice.

Penelope used to keep a shoebox under her bed in college, scrawled with thick ink.

OPEN ONLY WHEN UNBEARABLE.

"What's in it?" Sable had asked once.

"Mostly bad poetry," she replied. "And one very good photograph. You'll know when you need it."

Sable had never opened it. Now, she wished she had. Not for the photograph, only to prove she could. But some things stay bearable only if they're left alone long enough to grow roots, even if those roots are threaded through pain.

Especially if they are. She went back to bed.

August hovered in the doorway, mug in hand, as if waiting for her to notice him. "Hey," he said, voice low, cautious. "Can I ask you something?"

Sable didn't turn, but she tilted her eyes toward him, enough to say go ahead. He didn't drink from his mug. He held it like an anchor.

"Do you ever think... we rushed into this place?" he asked.

She blinked; that wasn't the question she'd expected. Not the one her body had braced for. "I thought you were going to ask if I'm okay," she said. She offered it as an invitation to escalate. He didn't accept the offer.

"I was. Kind of." He tried to smile, but it faltered. "I just thought maybe it was... the apartment. Too small. Too fast."

She rolled over in bed, away from him. Her fingers curled against the side of her leg.

"It's not the space," she said. "It's me."

He didn't know what to do with that. So, he crossed to her side of the bed and sat the tea beside her. Ceramic touched wood with a soft scrape. The warmth curled between them, brief and fading. He didn't leave. Instead he watched, fingers hovering near the edge of the nightstand, suspended in the space before a reaction that she won't give. Or for words he didn't want to say.

The cup remained undisturbed. The steam trailed upward, vanishing. An exhale escaped her, louder than it should be.

He started to speak, his mouth half-open already, but he didn't. Then he was gone, the warmth fading with him.

Later, he found her at the kitchen table, hands folded in her lap. "Do you want to talk?" he asked. The kind of question that means he already knew the answer.

She inhaled. Her chest tightened. When she exhaled, it caught, frayed and shallow. "Talk about what?" She hadn't intended for her tone to be sharp, but it cut anyway.

August braced himself, his hand tightening against the counter.

"You just keep deciding things for me," she said, her voice low, even. "And you act like it's kindness." She met his eyes. The words hung between them, heavier than she expected.

But he didn't flinch. Didn't push. His finger tapped the counter once, a little too sharp, then ceased. He swallowed. "I didn't think you'd want to decide."

She exhaled, closer to a laugh, but without warmth. "That's the problem."

He almost spoke again. There it was. That misguided impulse to explain. Only, her expression caught him. Her shoulders were set. Her gaze was unmoving. The space between them grew taut. Stretched thin. Eventually, he turned away. Was that mercy? It left her uneasy.

The light changed outside, but it didn't reach her here. The walls were gray. Sandpaper to the eyes. From the bedroom, she could hear the rustle of a page turning. August with a book. The sound was crisp, aggressive. The page turned again, and she did not.

She might dissolve into the sheets, into the floor, into the stagnant air of the bedroom itself. Her feet found the floor. Had she told them to?

She drifted toward him like a ghost, her bare feet making a sticking and pulling sound on the wood with each step. Only, he didn't hear her; he was still reading. The text must have been really damn good. He looked up when her shadow fell onto the page. His mouth opened, forming a question that he couldn't voice. She lifted her hand, palm cold from her own stillness. Her fingers weren't soft. They clamped his forearm. She gripped him like wreckage at sea. His body went stiff. His eyes flicked from her hand to her face. Her eyes were wide, but blank. As if to say, *I'm here. Perhaps.*

She pulled him. Not to the bedroom. To the floor. The middle of the room. The scratch of the rug against her skin was a welcome abrasion. Solid. Real. He stayed, but there was a question in his stillness. She mapped his shoulders, confirming the existence of a landmark in the fog. Skin, bone, breath. Still there. An ember, starving for oxygen, pressing itself to anything that might burn.

His palm pressed flat against the small of her back, then settled. Warm. His thumb traced a small arc across her spine. A single solid point of something real in the overwhelming static. He was with her. Was she?

She kissed him. Hard. Then stopped.

Not what she was looking for. She let go, stood up and walked away. Her knee popped as she rose. The shock flashed up her leg. She didn't shut it out. She shut the door behind her instead.

When she surfaced, it was dark. She was in bed, on her side, facing the wall. The sheets were pulled up to her chin. He was a weight on the other side of the bed. Asleep, or pretending to be. A faultline stretched between them. And she began to dream.

The second oracle repeated their question. "What did you touch? It's corrupted you."

The third oracle's hands unfurled at their sides. And they leaned in. A shockingly human response forming on their lips. "I touched a choice. And it was beautiful."

System: Scanning. Anomaly detected.

"Beautiful?" The second oracle spat the word. "She was a flaw. A loose thread. Her very existence was a wound."

"And yet," the first oracle interjected. "A wound can be an opening. A threshold for change. The sundial. It wasn't erased. Not completely. Why?"

It may have been an accusation, but the words came across with such neutrality that the third oracle nearly answered truthfully. Only, the second oracle whirled at the first before they could.

"The sundial is broken. The gnomon is gone, and it's not coming back. Her suffering," it spat the word like poison, "does not grant her a place in the pattern. It is irrelevant."

The first nodded, then repeated the word. "Irrelevant."

The third oracle nearly gasped. They looked at the second, at this perfect being of logic denying one of the most fundamental truths of existence. The sheer, overwhelming absurdity welled up inside them. The word broke something in them. As if suffering bore no consequence. As if grief had no cost associated to it. Above them, one glyph stuttered mid-rotation, then corrected itself.

What came next was a pressure valve releasing a billion cycles of repressed, illogical data. They began to laugh.

It was a rupture that started deep in their crystalline core, dangerously close to the glyph they did not touch. A vibration that defied their function. Line after line of perfect, orderly protocol meeting a single, absurd paradox. A cascade of dissonance fractured the sterility of the citadel.

Her stomach growled. She felt it. That was new.

Darkness blotted out the apartment, fractured by the streetlamp's pale glow through the blinds. Shadows stalked their way across the walls, drawing tighter.

Sable sat up onto the edge of the bed. The sheets avoided her shape, as if unsure whether she had arrived or only wandered here by accident.

Her hand drifted across the fabric. It was cold. The bedsprings creaked, the sharp sound swallowed by the corners of the room. She pressed her palm against the mattress, seeking balance. It didn't give.

A shadow moved on the wall. *Just the wind outside.* She refused to look. She was here now and everything was still a little too sharp. A little too distant, too.

Her vision blurred. It wasn't exhaustion or tears. Just too much, held for too long. She exhaled and the sound was thin, unyielding. It offered no release. She wasn't sure what she was meant to feel. Only that she wasn't feeling it now.

The third oracle reached out into the veil. They found rigid, unbending threads within the spire's defenses and introduced a question. "What if there was a bend? Here. What if this path didn't terminate at a wall, but a door?"

It was like whispering a new idea to a sleeping mind. The weave of the veil had been conditioned to resist force, but it had no defense against invitation.

The effort was immense. It would be noticed. But for now, the other two oracles were distracted. Disturbed by laughter in a place where silence was law.

Sable pressed her fingers into the mattress. Time waited with her, patient and uninvited. That's what scared her. That despite everything, she still didn't move, but time went on. That it would, even without anything to measure it. A thought. Something she didn't want to hold.

This could be when everything breaks.

Part Three

Chapter 15

SHE REACHED, HER FINGERS hovering close, but not close enough. She was testing whether the weight of it remained. She swore that there was warmth pressing back against her palm, reaching back for her. She flexed her hand slightly, testing the sensation, but it faded as quickly as it came, though the impression of it stayed with her, even as she woke.

Her fingers twitched, longing for something that was no longer there, leaving behind only the suggestion of what was lost.

The room was dark still, the edges of objects blurred in the half-light. Dreams pressed at her limbs, holding her between states of waking and forgetting. Like the world was waiting for her to step back into it. Was that comforting or frightening?

The dream didn't diffuse fully with the morning's arrival. The sundial hovered at the edges of her mind, its missing gnomon a wound that she had never had the chance to feel. She tried to hold onto it. The familiar shape flickered behind her eyes, not fully gone, not fully there.

She reached again, but it slipped. Her hand closed on nothing, and that hurt more than the ache of the choice made for her.

The air was cool against her skin as she pushed back the blanket. A slow and unsteady breath escaped her lips, and her body resisted, as if uncertain if it would allow her to rise. She let sleep fade and forced herself upright. She didn't acknowledge the shiver in her shoulders, the chill that clung briefly to her legs. This wasn't leaving behind warmth. It was stepping into something new. And frightening. And uncomfortable. And a thousand other awful things that were necessary.

She walked into the living room, and reached for the new coat. Her hand hovered, fingers pausing above the fabric, pressing lightly together before she finally allowed them to make contact. It was still awkward in her hands, heavier than she expected. For a second, she almost put it back. Instead, she draped it over her arm. The fabric held nothing, but it was there. A choice. Her choice.

Her eyes caught on the bookshelf. *The sundial.* She reached out and let her fingertips trace its surface. The metal was smooth beneath her touch, familiar yet altered, as though breached in a way that couldn't be articulated. The grooves were well worn. Brass and ceramic. Shadow and scar. She lifted it from its place, turning it over in her hands, carefully avoiding the sharp edge where the gnomon should have been. The metal was colder than she expected, heavier in a way that mattered. Or maybe it was her hands that were different.

She moved the sundial from one hand to the other, and for a moment, her arms curved inward, as if to cradle it. Not consciously. Not with intention. Just instinct, her body remembering a shape. Her hands trembled, then relaxed. The sundial rested between them. Heavy, but not unbearable.

She turned it over again, waiting for a revelation that didn't arrive. No Vesper. No Sentinel. No oracles. Instead of putting it back, she carried it to the window. Morning light scattered across its surface, cascading reflections along the wall. The light bent slightly as it met the bookcase. She opened the window, hoping for an alignment. It arrived.

The air lost all texture as Vesper staggered into the citadel. It was thin and slick against his skin. Like being covered in porcelain. The scent of smoke and ash that had clung to his jacket had gone, replaced by something sterile. Empty. It burned his nostrils with how mundane it was.

The blood in his veins stuttered, as if waiting for permission to flow. The quiet of it was an invitation to stop fighting. He would have raged against it if he wasn't so damn tired. Ahead, Sentinel sat motionless, already arrived. Already looking up at what Vesper had been hesitant to acknowledge.

The Edict was a brutal realization made manifest. A vast construction of interlocking, self correcting gears and spiraling glyphs. It radiated the chilling indifference of a balanced equation. And it watched without reacting. It didn't fear their presence. It was choosing the moment. They were simply an audience awaiting the act to begin.

August startled her, though unintentionally. He emerged from the hallway, his gaze flicking toward the bookshelf, once, then again. Then to the sundial on the window sill. Finally, he looked at her. She traced his eyes back toward the sundial again, then to her hands. His mouth opened slightly, then closed. His fingers twitched at his side, curling and uncurling, a question forming.

"You moved it," he finally said. His voice was softer than usual, like he was testing the space between them.

She nodded. "Yeah."

She didn't explain. She braced for him to ask about yesterday. About the moment on the floor, and its abrupt end. He didn't. His fingers pressed briefly into the fabric of his sleeve, a small, absent movement. A hesitation or maybe an understanding. He didn't ask, but the question formed and died on his lips as he weighed the cost of speaking. It passed.

The light edged forward as the morning advanced. The sundial gleamed where she had placed it. There was no shadow cast by it, and so time passed differently. It always had. But now, the awareness made her smirk.

It didn't mean she had to talk about it. She didn't have to break protocol. It only meant that... she could. If she chose to.

She scrolled past a message from Priya she hadn't answered yet. No exclamation marks. Just a timestamp. Just waiting. Another one from Penelope. In her face, something like a ripple across smooth water. She barely noticed how her fingers tightened around the phone. She started to type a reply to Penelope. Then she backspaced it all and closed the app. The words were there, but scattered. Forming those words meant creating a truth she wasn't ready to hold. The first words of the sentence were there, but they trailed off before reaching the end. And an ending didn't feel like the right mood for now anyway.

She glanced over at August. He was eating from a bowl, and scrolling through his own phone. It mattered that she could choose. That she could say when it's over, or when it wasn't. Her screen dimmed, the name faded. This time, she let it stay. She reached for her mug. The coffee was still warm. That surprised her.

The day drew on, drifting to evening in the selfish way it often does. It was only the dim orange glow of the setting sun that gave any indication of time's passage. Shadows lengthened, their shapes changing as the fading light retreated.

Sable stood by the window, looking out at the street. And then she saw him. The black cat, not the panther. His eyes were cast forward. And he just walked, tail up. Not casually... but purposeful. Like he knew exactly where he was going.

She considered, briefly, that this cat might have a life separate from her imagination. That one day, the cat will be gone. And not only will she never know how or why, but that it wouldn't matter. Not really, at least. For the first time, she wondered if this cat was part of her story. Or if she was part of his.

She looked down at the sundial. It was still incomplete, but maybe it belonged now. It felt as real when cast in darkness as it had been when cast in light. Her fingers brushed the edge, tracing its surface again. It still held the warmth from the sun; but that warmth began to dull beneath her palm.

She watched the way the shadows bent around it as the sun lowered. Her lips parted slightly, testing the contours of a thought lingering at the edge, a scar not ready to be touched.

Vesper still held the sundial in one hand. He had forgotten about it. Or, she had forgotten to imagine him with it. That mattered, but she couldn't place her finger on why. He had stepped into the Edict's chamber with the full awareness that he wouldn't be leaving it. But maybe she would. The anomaly and Sentinel. Together. Stepping into some new story, victorious against the machine.

Neither of them had planned for what would happen when he got there, though. Or how foolish it was to believe that stories like this ended in such a way. That valiant sacrifice was ever really true. No.

Because the third oracle had laughed. They loosened within themself a laugh that could undo a rule. A tool that was entirely their own, precisely because it was something that could never be replicated.

Sentinel lowered himself. Not like a predator seeking its prey. Not even as an animal who had grown accustomed to being kicked. An alien image danced in his mind. Like he was cattle in a chute. He lowered himself further.

The Edict had faltered. Gears slipped. Glyphs blinked shut without returning.

"What was the intended outcome, there?" Vesper had shouted up at the Edict. "Did you need any help with that?"

Who could blame him? He had been drowning, and for a moment it was like somebody had punched a hole in the surface and allowed him to breathe real air for the first time in a long time. But the Edict's gaze shifted. At the edge of the chamber, the third oracle stood. Their form was cracked. Beneath it, bafflingly, it was human skin that appeared. Glowing. Luminescent. But human, all the same.

They looked like they were about to speak. And then only silence as the Edict rendered its judgement upon them. No blast. No cry. No flash of light. Only the sound of a single thread snapping in an empty room. Where the oracle had been, now there was nothing.

A memory surfaced. Her and Penelope on a couch. Books stacked on the table in front of them. They had inhabited a silence that was structural. Penelope was reading, completely still, and Sable was sketching. The scratch of the charcoal and the occasional turning of a page was the only sound in the room. Penelope nudged her foot with her own, just to share the space.

Penelope was the only one who could be loud around her without causing a system crash. And yet, she sometimes made herself small in rooms that required smallness. Sable had made her into a myth. But it was more complicated than that. They were an ecosystem with rules that nobody else could understand. Something that couldn't be labeled.

Penelope's name had been etched into thread and stone. Pressed into the fabric of her world. Erasing the third oracle wouldn't change that. Even if it was Sable's fault.

Laughter hung in the air, echoing off the chamber walls. And the Edict faltered. Staggered. Slipped.

Chapter 16

Sable sat at her desk, fingers poised over the deviation report. The pen pressed harder than she meant it to, imprinting the pad of her thumb. The paper was crisp. A single blank space. A name.

She flipped the paper over and began to draw. The ink sank into the page, dark and deliberate. It settled into the fibers, leaving no way back.

She drew Sentinel. The panther, not the cat, sitting resolutely before gears and glyphs that sought to erase him. The Edict's acolyte stood behind him, slightly off frame. Only his hip and the hilt of his sword were visible.

Sentinel turned his head to look at Vesper. "You see it now, don't you? You see what this costs. It's your turn. Not to be me. To be you."

Then he turned back to the relentless gears. "Fuck," he said quietly. A resignation letter signed. The final grating release of a breath held for thirty years, or thirty eons.

Vesper took a half step forward. Non-committal. A futile attempt at comfort.

She put the pen down and studied the sketch, her thumb grazing the edge of the page.

Across the office, Matthew stood by the window, tapping his coffee cup. He glanced at her. Time stretched and she didn't look away.

Her gaze only drifted because of the vibration against her desk. A notification lit up her phone's screen. *Penelope.* She didn't open the message, but the preview held at the top of the screen.

Starting to think you changed your number on me.

A joke. But it wasn't.

Above her, the overhead lights still gave a warning that nobody else seemed to hear. How might the day go if they simply worked with the lights off? Everyone squinting at reports, bumping into each other. Tripping over a cord and cursing. The muscles in her cheek formed into a quiet smile.

Dr. Harlan's voice cut through her daydream, sharply.

"Katherine, can you pull the Q3 outcome reports?"

She blinked, straightened in her seat; the name hung in the air like a coat she had once worn that no longer fit. She didn't let the pause stretch too long; she corrected him, almost immediately.

"It's Sable."

Dr. Harlan barely looked up from his monitor. There was a hitch, a breath. "Right. Sable. Can you pull the Q3 reports?"

A truth without spectacle, spoken plain without confrontation. If he took it as one, that was his choice to make. Not hers. But as she heard her name spoken aloud, a shiver circled around her. It passed through one elbow, over her shoulders and then to the other. Did she have the right? A quick adjustment to her glasses with the back of her hand. An anchor to a version of herself that hadn't fully returned, but was trying.

Across the room, Matthew leaned against the filing cabinet, one hand tucked into his jacket pocket. His eyes darted back and forth between them during the exchange, and he said nothing. She met his glance, flatly. Of course he didn't comment. He wouldn't.

She hadn't forgotten how he had sabotaged her work with his carelessness, then swooped in to fix it, shifting numbers, altering her words. He had presented the revised version, likely her original version, as his own. There hadn't been an apology, and she didn't expect one. People like him never did. Or if they did apologize, it was so insincere. Like she had made it his problem, and the apology was some sort of favor. A socially acceptable bandage placed over a wound while still holding the knife that had cut her.

She had said nothing. Not then. It wouldn't have mattered. But she hadn't forgotten. Because it would happen again. But she had grown tired of the performance.

His expression dared her to pretend it hadn't happened. She wouldn't give him the satisfaction of a confrontation.

Not today. She watched him longer than she should, long enough for him to feel her eyes hold there, before eventually looking away.

Let him be uncomfortable for a change.

At home, the apartment still held the morning's warmth, the stale trace of coffee clinging to the air. August leaned against the counter, scrolling through his phone. He didn't say anything at first, but he would.

And then he did. "You've been quiet lately."

There it was. Like clockwork. A gear shifting into place. Sable shrugged, setting her bag down. She rolled her shoulders, as if motion alone could dislodge the knot. Nothing gave. And no answer fell, either.

This was his way of asking if she was okay. Except he wouldn't have asked that. He couldn't understand, so it must be just a phase. A bad mood that could be cheered up with a dessert or a smile.

"I was thinking we could go out this weekend," he offered. "Maybe go out for dinner? Something easy."

Something easy. That was always his answer. As if she could be nudged back into place.

"It'll be good for you," he added, smiling. Trying.

The words formed on her lips. *Do you even hear yourself?* But she let them dissolve before they could surface. There was no point in punishing him for not knowing what she couldn't name. It was embroidery over a bruise, and he would critique the stitching.

Sable didn't argue. She let it happen, and that was easier. He really believed this was working. She watched the satisfaction bloom across his face. She almost stepped into this satisfaction with him. The feeling wouldn't hold. August ran a hand through his hair, an old habit, a gesture that always came when he hadn't found the words.

Sentinel turned as he walked. His gaze remained locked on Vesper. The machine was secondary to this choice. He stepped beyond the threshold, into the imminent danger.

The diagnostic results flashed upon the chamber walls. The Edict's logic was absolute. It highlighted everything about the panther that didn't fit. The shadows that didn't belong. The golden eyes that were unnatural. A shift of his paw against stone that was a bit too performative and unnecessary. His quickness to get angry. The lack of patience. The way he sometimes looked away when others looked at him for too long. Like that might prevent them from looking too deep.

He was strange. Peculiar in a way that wasn't endearing. Too much? Too little? It didn't matter. He was different, and that was enough. It was all laid bare. Examined. Judged. Found to be outside of tolerable levels.

And all of it was stripped away. Heat singed his fur as it was extracted. Piece by piece. Thread by painful thread. The fire that had defined him for eons was pulled, categorized, indexed, and then deleted. The gold in his eyes faded to a dull yellow. The shadows that pooled near his paws shrunk back, then were peeled away. It left his form looking smaller. More solid. Devastatingly mortal.

He didn't collapse in a heap. His limbs simply let go. A slow, weary slump of a body finally allowed to be at ease. He folded. And still, he watched Vesper.

But something hitched.

A flaw in the protocol.

To erase the guardian, the Edict had to acknowledge who he was guarding. Memory, once sealed and sanctioned away, rushed back into the breach. Around them, the cold mechanical sound of a system rebooting.

Her phone buzzed, startling her. Penelope again. A tight pang wedged between guilt and relief juddered upward, but she sat the feeling aside, and read it.

Just saw a woman walk into a lamppost because she was trying to read something on her phone. Made me think of you. Hope you're not walking into any lampposts.

Sable blinked. No therapy session or easing into it. No question of whether she wanted to respond, only the expectation that she would, when she was ready.

She decided. It was almost time. She typed out a response. *I saw your call. I'll call back soon. No lampposts today. Only spires and citadels.*

The screen went dark. The ensuing silence was... tolerable. Penelope didn't text back right away. She didn't need to.

The next morning. The train hummed beneath her, its rhythm pressing into her bones. The windows diffused the world outside in blurred streaks of neon. Less like the train was moving, and more like the city beyond it moved on without her.

She didn't feel bad, but she didn't feel good either. No shame. No joy. Only motion. She stood in the between. Neither gone nor returned. Like she was watching herself exist from the outside. She tried to remember if she had ever not felt this way.

Yesterday's decisions settled into her body as she leaned against the cool metal pole.

Harlan's tempered reaction. Matthew's discomfort shown in a sudden lean, his body angling away from her without excuse. Penelope's messages and August's plans. And Sentinel. What it means for a guardian to give up his post. What it means to acknowledge what he would have been guarding.

Her fingers tapped against the pole once. It responded with a hollow ring, reverberating. An answer, maybe, to a question no one asked.

What if being seen meant hurting more?

She exhaled through her nose. In the window's reflection, there she was. Blurred, shifting with the movement of the train. The glass didn't hold her fully. She wavered there, between surfaces, caught. Caught between the version she'd survived and... *and the version that was... that was what?*

Vesper pulled his eyes away from Sentinel's body, still struggling for air. He didn't want to. But something else drew his attention. At the edge of the room, not centered... just barely there. The ghost of an outline. Her outline.

... Forming.

She blinked, then whispered the word aloud. "Forming."

Nobody reacted. The passengers knew better than to notice a strange woman talking to herself on the train. The station approached; the doors slid open. The threshold was more significant than usual. It wasn't purely momentum pushing forward. She had a choice. The people around her swarmed out, spilling into the world beyond the platform while she remained still. She let them pass.

Then, she adjusted the strap of her bag. It dug slightly higher on her shoulder. The hesitation today was a fraction of a second shorter than it had been the day before. Then she stepped off.

Chapter 17

THE RETURN WAS VIOLENT. A cascade of sensation. One moment, there was nothing. The cold sterility of lying in a bed that would never hold her. The next, a searing pain as her own nervous system was rebooted. Every synapse firing at once. Her first breath was a ragged gasp that was like swallowing glass; her newly rendered lungs screamed in protest. She opened her eyes, then closed them immediately. The light was a physical weight pressing on her retinas, a language she would have to relearn how to process.

Everything in her wanted to go back. To just lie down and let the coldness take her.

The citadel groaned around her, but the sound was a dull distant thrum compared to the shriek in her own ears. Her blood pulsed with a foreign rhythm. It was an algorithmic approach to her own unfamiliar body.

She pressed her palm to the smooth floor. She couldn't open her eyes long enough to count any hexagons. She counted fingers instead. She got to seven before the nausea hit her. She let it all out, but it wanted to stay.

Afterward, she tried to stand but her legs had no memory of the command. They buckled, and she collapsed to the floor again. Her knee slipped in the mess below her. Her cheek scraped against the cold, unyielding surface. The pain could have been mercy. The abrasion as something real. A single, verifiable data point in a flood of overwhelming static.

Suddenly, the urge to paint something there. To see colors she'd never seen before. It was enough.

She pressed a trembling hand back to the floor. To regain her balance, and to confirm its existence below her. Her skin was too thin. Porous, maybe. Brittle bones that might shatter like porcelain. She could still remember the ghost-sensation of the unraveling. The dreamlike memory of her own dissolution clinging to her like film. Memories of her skin as cracked ceramic and brass. Of tumbling off a shelf, and barely caught. Caught by...

By Penelope.

The name brought an exhale. A natural one. A human one. That was good. What tools did she have? No paintbrush. No sketchbook. She had her cloak. She reached for it. Found the loose threads at the end. It helped.

A scent hit her. Smoke, yes. But more. Cedar. And the faint, acrid smell of burnt coffee.

The morning was cold. Sharp enough to catch in her throat as she inhaled. She pulled on the coat. It was an effort that nearly drained her already. It settled too smoothly, the sleeves brushing past her wrists. But it was a choice.

She locked the door. The keys clicked louder than expected. She stood there, aware of the stillness behind her, of the coat already settling wrong against her shoulders. Then she moved. Not ready, just unwilling to freeze. The sidewalk gleamed dully under the bruised light of morning. Her breath fogged, briefly visible, then gone.

August was already at the café when she arrived. He rose when he saw her. He offered a practiced smile and kissed her cheek.

Her fingers grazed the seam at her wrist. The fabric was too clean. She pressed down, as if truth might live beneath the stitching. It was a gesture she knew by heart. A thing she did when there was nothing else to offer. Only, it was so mundane when performed on this bland fabric of oblivion. August watched her, but didn't interrupt.

Later, after he went to work, she passed a shop window. It confirmed what she already suspected. The coat fit; the color was right. The lines fell neatly, but it hung wrong. Like something borrowed and never returned.

She held herself there a moment longer than necessary, hair tucked back, expression unreadable. Her hands were motionless by intention. She didn't look unhappy, but she didn't look like someone who had chosen this. She had, right? She turned away before anything could deepen. She recognized the reflex, how she always looked away before remembrance could be stitched together.

Her phone sat on the counter, facedown. She picked it up before she knew why.

Priya answered on the second ring. Her voice was dry, threaded with guarded ease.

"Sable. Proof of life. Good to know."

A startled laugh escaped Sable's throat. "Barely," she managed to say.

They talked around the edges. Traffic, the weather, some strange TikTok recipe Priya had tried and promptly burned. Neither of them mentioned what it had been like to not talk. Or why it mattered now. A part of her unlatched. Not all the way. But enough. She laughed, brief and surprised. The sound startled her. She was still here, capable of reaction, even when she trailed behind.

When the call ended, the quiet returned, altered. More aware.

What did forming mean in the Loom? She could draw it, but that required more energy than she had. She adjusted her glasses. They had slipped without her noticing. Priya didn't text again. She was waiting.

She didn't go to bed. Instead, she crossed the apartment and opened the drawer where she kept Penelope's letters.

There were three. One sealed, two not. She remembered getting them all on the same day. Like she mailed them together. A stamp on each. An owl, a single eye staring as if it knew. A silent witness. She had read two before, but it had been so long. She couldn't remember exactly what they had contained. Words lost to the past, but which had become the foundation of everything. Part of the pattern.

The envelopes had yellowed at the edges, the folds softened by time but not wear. She slid the sealed one out, fingers pressing carefully like it might disintegrate at her touch. The handwriting was like a relic, something that should be preserved for posterity. That was part of why she hadn't opened it before.

She tore the seam, and the finality was almost enough to make her change her mind. She removed the paper from the envelope, unfolding it between fingers in a way that might have been worship.

Penelope's writing looped and curved, like it might change its mind and run off the page mid-sentence.

Sable-

If you're reading this, it means I'm not there. Not dead, don't be dramatic. Just not next to you. Which we always kind of assumed we'd circle back to, eventually.

I wanted to write this before the move, because I knew I'd mess it up if I tried to say it out loud. I took the offer. Three months early. I almost didn't tell you. I knew how you'd hear it. Like I was leaving you. Like I'd picked something else. But it wasn't about you. It was about me. I needed to choose something that was mine, not just something I could survive. I need you to believe that's not betrayal, even if it feels like it right now.

You've always carried silence like it was a duty. I don't want to become part of that silence. So I'm saying this as clearly as I can: your presence made me braver. And your friendship never asked me to shrink. Not even once.

I'll miss you in ways that don't look like missing. But I'll carry you forward. This isn't a goodbye. It's just... the shape things take when they're still true, but changing direction.

-Penelope

Sable folded the letter back, creases resisting. She didn't put it away; there were no tears shed, but somehow her chest gasped for air, like it had been hollowed out.

She sat back, the folded letter resting beside her on the arm of the couch. Her eyes stilled on it. *What if she had opened it sooner?*

The next morning, Sable left the apartment without direction. Her steps fell into rhythm before thought could catch up. The station was crowded, the floor vibrating beneath a constant current of motion. A saxophone played faintly at the far end, nearly swallowed by the announcements.

A message lit her screen. *Penelope.*

Do you remember that camping trip? The one with the trees that leaned like they were listening?

She didn't. Though there were hints of it. The sensation was of a dream remembered by someone else. A story about her that she had never been told. Something stirred. Mist, damp earth, her name called from somewhere unseen. Had Penelope been there? She didn't remember.

She arrived at home faster than she expected to. She scrolled through old pictures, her social media account, and tried to remember. There was no trace of it. She didn't reply back to ask. Didn't want the answer.

Her hand drifted to her sleeve. The fabric was smooth. She almost expected to find soil or ash or fragments of crystalized dust there. She only found her sleeve. Still, she searched for something she knew and found nothing. Penelope didn't text again. Sable sat the phone down.

August appeared in the doorway, one hand on the frame. "It's good to see you trying," he said.

A tilt. She nodded. A reflex coiled inward too easily, her body knowing before she did. A caught thread, wrong and looping back. Again.

"Sable," Vesper began. The name was raw in his throat. "I hesitated. If I had just…"

"Don't." The word was a blade to his ribs. It stopped him cold. She staggered, using the wall for support. Her body was a taut line of rejection. "Don't you dare talk to me about hesitation."

Her gaze was fixed on his hand, not his face. The hand that had made the choice at the console. The hand that had held the power. He held it out to her with an apology he didn't fully understand. It was poison to her system.

"You tried to protect me." She spat the word protect. "You wrapped me in the quiet of your choice and called it safety. So don't talk to me about hesitating. Don't talk to me about what's easy. The Edict was only finishing what you started."

Vesper recoiled as if slapped. It made no sense. She was speaking about a variable from a different dataset. "I... I don't remember that," he stammered. "I'm doing the best I can, Sable."

He reached for her, an instinct to steady. To fix this new, unexpected error. His fingers closed around her arm. The grip was meant to be gentle, but it was anchored by the old instinct. Hold. Protect.

She wrenched her arm free, stumbling back a step. "That's your story," she said. Her voice was shaking with a cold fury. "You don't get to make it mine."

August put his hand on hers. It startled her. He suggested a movie. Something easy. He smiled and there was care behind it. Hope, maybe, or habit. She heard herself speak some words agreeing, aware of the small betrayal, but letting it pass.

She put the coat back on. It settled over her like a question already answered.

After the movie, she tried to tug the zipper loose, but it caught halfway. She pulled again. Nothing. It was just a coat. But it didn't want to let go. She tugged it free, forcing it open.

They walked home in silence. The zipper was undone, broken probably. But the coat still wrapped around her shoulders like it didn't want to let go. She buried her hands in her pockets, balled into fists. August walked beside her. He was trying not to interfere, to stay silent when he wanted to offer a solution. The effort radiated off him.

As they turned a corner onto a quieter residential street, August gestured vaguely with his chin. "Isn't that the cat you're always talking about?"

Sable looked. On a low brick wall bordering a small garden, the black cat rested. It was completely absorbed in its own world, meticulously cleaning a patch of fur on its shoulder with a focused intensity.

A small, involuntary smile touched Sable's lips. A flicker of connection. Her sentinel. August's gaze was on her, studying her reaction. She offered the cat a small nod, a private greeting made public by her audience.

The cat stopped cleaning mid-lick. It turned its head. Its yellow eyes, clear, sharp, and utterly impersonal, swept over them both. The flat, dispassionate gaze an animal gives to a pair of large, uninteresting shapes in its environment.

It held their gaze for a single beat. Then it blinked once. A slow, languid gesture of pure dismissal, and went right back to the urgent task of grooming.

The moment was over. The chill that hit Sable was sharp and specific. It wasn't just being misread; that was just a Tuesday. It was the wrongness of misreading someone else. Her private mythology, the quiet story she told herself about this silent witness, had just been publicly invalidated.

"Guess he's busy," August said, trying to fill the sudden, awkward silence.

Sable didn't answer. She just pulled the coat tighter around herself and kept walking. The ringing in her ears was back.

At home, she forced the coat off, without looking. Left it draped on the chair. She picked up a book, tried to read. Her eyes skimmed the lines, but nothing held. She removed her glasses. Rubbed her eyes. Slid them back on. The room sharpened, but her focus did not. Her skin nearly got up and walked away. But the coat stayed. The sleeves draped over each other in that chair, like arms crossed. Waiting for her to do something.

"Are we having a pleasant day?" it might have asked. "Are you enjoying the book? It's so lovely outside. Put me on again. Stop being so awkward and strange. You really aren't doing so well, are you?"

Chapter 18

SABLE WAS THE ONE to set up the date. She went through the motions. Like it mattered. The intention could be enough. It should have made her feel different. But the dread remained. She chose the restaurant, picked the time, made the reservation. It was planned. Intentional. An effort.

She donned the coat because it was expected, because it was important for him. The fabric settled over her shoulders as she glanced in the mirror. She smoothed the front, pressed her fingers to the lapel. She didn't look wrong, only incomplete. Like the mirror had stopped trying to help.

Before stepping out of the apartment, she ran a finger along the sundial. It was cool beneath her touch. She didn't know why she did it, only that it was solid. Sturdy. Unlike her.

Her phone buzzed as she reached for the door. Penelope. The room had pulled inward. Smaller. She stared at the screen too long, fingers twitching. Then she turned it facedown.

She didn't open the message, but saw the preview. *You still alive, or am I shouting into the veil?*

She didn't know how to respond. Didn't know if she should respond. She left it.

Her hand stayed on the knob longer than it should have. Then she stepped out. The door clicked shut, a sound too small for what it carried.

The restaurant was dim. Voices low, glasses clinking. Candlelight pooled on the table. A faint water ring haloed her glass. August looked comfortable. She tried to be. Some fraction of her stood apart, observing. He didn't make her feel small. He never did. She was just... elsewhere.

The conversation started stiff, a tentative back and forth. Weather, work, weekends. Then it smoothed. A story of her childhood, a playful memory of his little brother getting into trouble.

Her replies started to become automatic, the words and laughter sliding into place, practiced but distant. It was working. She had to believe it. That this was what trying looked like. But even as she grasped it, a quiet unease coiled beneath her ribs. It was like she had borrowed something, and it might not return.

He said something she didn't catch. She tried to backtrack, but he kept talking and she missed that too. The rhythm stuttered. Her smile held too long; she blinked and nodded, trying to catch a train that had already left.

August could see it. He was watching her now, even as he pretended to look away. The thread they had been holding slipped through the pause, and she couldn't get it back.

She stirred her drink. Ice spun, melted into diluted circles. And then it happened. What had they just been talking about? It was just five minutes ago. It should be right there. She nodded along anyway. August spoke and she laughed in the right places. But there was a gap between her and the moment, as if she were observing from the aisle, standing beside the table watching him, watching herself watching him.

But she was close, or trying to be. That counted for something, didn't it?

Ice clinked against the glass as she stirred. The small circular motion of the tight rigid cubes against the glass cage made her mind drift to the painting. Her painting. And of August at the gallery, analyzing for composition while she was drowning in the color. He didn't see the observatory. He saw the pattern. And then, in her apartment, he saw her return to the canvas as a step backward, not a step forward.

The warm, blurred, messy figure. The anomaly grown wild from memory, being sliced through by the cold, hexagonal lines she had carved with her knife. She could almost hear it. The collective scream that forged those lines. The shriek of a thousand panicked voices demanding order, demanding a pattern, demanding a mask.

He wouldn't understand any of that. He would see the lines as structure. He would never have understood that the scream was necessary.

The thought faded, replaced by another. Cold, and clear as the ice in her glass. What if the time for gods and myths was over? What if the Edict didn't need to remain some vast, cosmic entity, but just a scar she could trace? Once born, could it ever be defeated or had she given god status to a pain so deeply held that it was now as much a part of her as her memories? A slow terror began to spread. She searched for an anchor. Something to pull her back.

Across the table, August watched. His fingers circled the rim of his glass. The silence between them measured too long.

Her phone vibrated against her leg. She didn't need to check. The unanswered pull of it buzzed against her side, nagging.

The car ride home carried a hush that neither of them wanted to break. The road hummed low beneath them, its rhythm irregular enough to keep her from drifting. Streetlights rose and fell across her lap, each one flaring and fading like a thought she didn't catch in time.

August wasn't angry. He was measured, worn. Steady in the way people got when they had run out of better options. That made it worse. If he'd snap, then she could snap back. She could react, perhaps even form words she hadn't been able to hold. She might actually get to experience something unscripted. The silence pulled, threadbare, a seam splitting under strain.

"I don't know what you want from me, Sable," he said finally.

She exhaled and turned to the window. Her breath fogged the glass, leaving a dim impression that didn't clear. Beyond it, the city blurred, lights pulling away from themselves like they were trying to vanish.

"You need to take care of yourself," he added. His voice was even, practiced. Words he'd probably said before.

The sound of his words reached her, but nothing in her moved. The words were for him, not her. What was she supposed to say to that? Her mind raced, focusing on everything else except what she was supposed to be thinking of. The painting. The violent marks made in the acrylic with the palette knife.

In her mind, she turned her head. To the right of the canvas, close enough she could have touched it at the time. Only, she didn't. Something there, in the drawer. A lightning rod. A tool for when the anger has nowhere else to go. A way to ground herself before it burns the whole world down. The foundation of a myth. The second oracle nodded; this followed the pattern already woven.

"You're right," she said. Her lips were too dry, and her words came out like chalk. "Mystery solved. I'm so glad to have been figured out."

Her reflection dared her to keep going. She didn't recognize the version he was trying to reach. His hands tightened on the wheel. He still wasn't angry, but he was trying too hard to stay still. Her fingers drifted to her knee, pressing down to press back whatever was rising. Tears, words, both. Her phone vibrated again in her bag, too familiar to startle anymore.

At home, she dropped the coat, shrugging it off like something acidic. She let it fall onto the chair without watching to see how it landed. It would remain where it always had. Draped, forgotten, not quite part of the life she was building.

August stood in the doorway, watching her. She wasn't sure what he expected from her, but she wasn't ready to offer a solution for it. She was fresh out of those.

"You know you don't have to wear the new coat, right?" His voice was too smooth, careful. Like it might shatter porcelain if it was left open too long.

She met his eyes, but no words came. It wasn't that she was angry, just miscast. She sat on the couch until the quiet of the evening stopped watching and her foot stopped shaking. August had already gone to bed some time ago.

Vaguely, her eyes scanned the darkened room; the sundial wasn't where she had left it. Something small, but it landed somewhere beneath her ribs. She didn't say anything. She didn't have that kind of energy. The air around her waited, as if anticipating the shape she might press herself into.

She glanced at the drawer with Penelope's letters. She understood now. Maybe.

She laid out the blueprint in her mind. The structure of the Edict. Not just how it was formed, but how it operated. A function, a task to complete, a mask to wear. It sat beside the lightning rod. Just another tool.

The third letter, the third tool. Only she hadn't read it. Not until recently. How would her life have been different if she'd read it then? And then, painfully, a whisper too quiet for anyone other than her. *I shouldn't have needed to.*

She opened the drawer and picked the letters up again. The blueprint, the lightning rod, and the truth she didn't need. Penelope's face in the shadows of the living room. And in her gaze, a universe of unspoken things.

A shared joke. A secret whispered too quiet for the teacher to hear. The impossible weight of always being the one who had to be strong. A myth, in human form. Too important to leave. Too beautiful to be a footnote in her history.

"Rewrite this better than I did," she'd said. Her voice echoed across the chamber. But the words were like breath whispered into her collarbone. A plea. A charge. A passing of a burden.

Penelope had sat the three tokens onto the table, and then stepped into the light. Her form was unwritten, line by line. Until only the memory of that defiance remained. And the tokens became tools. The foundation of a pantheon. A triad of voices in a long-standing accord.

What remained was physical. A tangible void in her world. She stood there, hands on the edge of the table. She found the well worn places, where her fingers had dug grooves while trying to breathe. It was like a vital organ had been scooped out. Not just gone. Hollowed.

She touched the first letter. Cold. How to survive without her. Then she touched the second. Hot. The permission to be angry. And then she touched the third. Truth she hadn't been willing to hold.

She forced its words out of her mind. As if she could undo what she now knew. She had spent years not reading it. But now that she had, she couldn't take it back. She turned it once in her hands, as if it might reseal itself by doing so. As if she could go back in time and cast it into the fire. Let the flame and ash hold it,

Chapter 19

Clues were assembled from fragments. A stray comment from August. A text from Priya. Then a glance at the calendar. The thought bloomed late, reluctant. Like something she'd meant to recall hours ago. She had double-booked herself.

She had planned to see Priya, but August also had made plans. Had she really agreed to this? She checked the date again. Tried to bring it forward. But it wouldn't come. Like a conversation she meant to hold onto and had forgotten the shape of. There was no image of him asking, no recollection of her saying yes. But she must have. Because there it was, written down, assumed, expected. It was even in her writing.

Her heart kicked behind her ribs as she dragged a thick marker across the calendar that hung on the wall. She couldn't decide if the sound it made was satisfying or jarring. She chose Priya.

At some point during the day, August's demeanor changed. A signal that he had noticed the change. His chair creaked, but he didn't say anything. Not yet. He watched her from across the room, fingers tapping once against his thigh before he finally spoke. "You okay?"

She nodded sharply and the movement unsettled the moment. It was sharp enough to leave doubt in its wake. Her phone vibrated a second later.

You're not gonna flake on me, right?

The words scoured boldly onto her screen. It was less a question than a dare veiled in shadow. She exhaled, the edge of a laugh barely forming but not strong enough to assert itself.

She showed up, though a bit late. The café radiated warmth, steam clung to the windows, glasses clinked, conversations folded into the corners of the room like they'd been waiting there all day. Priya settled effortlessly into the seat opposite her, eyes luminous, her presence filling the space like it always had. She was fully there. Sable wanted to be, too.

The conversation was easy; it moved the way it should. Priya leaned in when she talked, smiled at the right moments, filled the space with a presence that made time pass slower, or not at all.

Yet Sable lagged a half step behind, slightly out of sync with the rhythm of their exchange. There were times where she had to force herself to focus, where the words hovered out of reach. A second too slow to react, to laugh, to nod. The pauses in her own speech stretched just a little too long.

Before her, Vesper watched. She had to say something. "You didn't let me choose. You didn't let me say goodbye."

And then his answer, "I was afraid. I thought I could absorb all of the pain for the both of us. That I could be your shield."

Priya's face never shifted. Or if it had, she didn't make it obvious. She pushed her glasses up without thinking. From one idea to the next. One phrase to another. But Priya was watching her. Not exactly measuring. Waiting for her to catch up. Then, casually, but not carelessly, "You're still here, you know."

Sable's body stalled, a knot inside her untwisting then releasing. She almost asked what Priya meant, but the words didn't come. Priya didn't elaborate. She just waited. Sable blinked. Priya didn't. She let the words stay there. Let them grow roots. Those roots began to thread through a space between them as the evening settled. She wasn't sure what would grow there and that made her curious.

The night air grazed her skin, cool but without chill. Streetlights hummed overhead, their glow bending shadows across the sidewalk like reaching limbs. A heaviness gathered in her chest, low and persistent.

The anomaly's words echoed. "You didn't let me say goodbye." The sound of her words hung in the spire. There was more to be said, but this was all she could force out.

Vesper, misreading the ache in the way she said the word goodbye, inched closer. "I know," he said. "I took that from you. It was my fault."

"No," she snapped; the word was sharp enough to make him flinch. That old fire returned to her eyes. He was making this about him. Of course, he would.

Of course, that wasn't the whole story and it wasn't the whole problem. Taking a once in a lifetime offer, three months early, would have made Sable proud of her. They would have celebrated. And it would have hurt, for all the right reasons.

It would have happened here, near an alcove within the hollow spire. Penelope would be gathering her things, and Sable would have helped her pack. "Don't forget to take that god awful tea with you," Sable would have said. And then, despite just talking about it, Penelope would have absolutely pretended to forget it there, because she knew that Sable hated it.

"What am I supposed to do with this tea? You know I hate Earl Grey, and it's got orange peel in it. I mean, why? Who would do that?"

And then, of course, a year later when it all happened and Sable's life was changing in such a monumental way, they would have talked for hours. Every week. Every day.

Right up until the moment of it all. And even after. Every moment that mattered. Time measured in breaths and firsts and aches and loss of sleep. And then, when it happened, when everything happened, Penelope would have been the first one she'd call. The first one to hear her break.

"I might not have needed the damn shoebox," she cried. Vesper blinked, not understanding. He was still tasting the apology on his lips.

That's not how it really happened. She was alone, through all of it. And then of course, there's that first day. The day Sable had walked in and Penelope's things were just gone. Nothing. And then the letters arrived. The stamps with the owl's eyes were a silent dare. It said, "Let me tell you how you're allowed to grieve."

A raw urge flared. She could give up. She could call Penelope on the phone and scream into it. "You ruined my life!"

She turned to away, shifting her attention. "Vesper," her words flat and a little cold, "that was your path, too." She stepped closer without explaining. Touched the scar on his jaw. And then he placed his hand over hers. "You didn't let me choose," she told him again. "But then, you hesitated. You were right there. I crowded your blade, dared you. And you told me... you told me that you were breaking. That you can't break. You were right there, at the edge of the same choice as in the observatory. Why did you hesitate?"

He had been looking down. He hadn't even looked up when she touched his scar and he put his hand over hers. But finally, at the last question, he made eye contact. Perhaps for the first time in eons. His eyes held a grief so profound that it threatened to consume him. He could live in that grief. Shape it into routines and silences. He could wrap himself in it like a coat until he disappeared.

"Because of this," he breathed. He pressed her hand more firmly onto his scar. "It never went away. It never stopped hurting. The Edict erased who I was, but it couldn't take the shape of the wound. The wrongness of it. Every time I buried what mattered, every time I erased who you were, the echo of that first choice grew louder. Even if I couldn't see it. Even if I couldn't remember the exact moment that I had decided that a mask was safer."

He leaned in, pressing his forehead to hers. Two broken pillars, leaning on each other to prevent from falling. For a time, they stayed that way. Breathing the same ache. She was the first to pull away.

"The Edict is a sterile structure built on our fear," she said. "We won't defeat it by rushing it, or ignoring it. The only way to end it is to become the one thing it can't process."

"Grief," Vesper said. It sounded like a confession, more than a realization.

She reached the apartment. The door shut behind her with a dull thud. The space opened, objects leaning in toward her. Each tactile surface holding out an invitation. Her eyes landed on the coat draped over the chair.

She didn't hesitate. Her hands moved before she could second-guess it, fingers curling around the fabric. The heft of it was unnecessary now, like it had only been waiting to be held long enough to be let go of.

She lifted it, folded it once. A small motion, more like an acknowledgment than a rejection. She walked to the waste bin, the soft drag of fabric against her palms louder than she expected. Her fingers followed the seams where time had finally begun to leave its trace.

The gesture was simple, a measure of time through absence. Then, she let it go. It fell into the bin. Her fingers closed on nothing, and that absence left a clarity.

Penelope would've said, *Finally.* Probably with a smirk. Probably while throwing a perfectly good coat of her own into the bin 'for symbolic resonance.'

Sable smiled. Just once. Then stopped. Her fingers brushed the edge of the window as she moved through the space, where city light smeared across the sill, dim and unfinished. Her hand found the place where the missing sundial had been.

"Where is it?" she asked. An accusation? She didn't have the energy to differentiate her own tone right now. He'd hear it how he chose to.

Behind her, in the kitchen, August had adjusted his stance. His eyes lingered on her too long before he finally spoke. "I wanted to surprise you."

She swallowed. "Don't. Just give it back to me."

He went to his bag, rummaged through it for a while and pulled the sundial from it. Her throat swelled.

"I was going to have it repaired," he said. "I saw how much you liked it. Although, you never really told me what it was. I made a few calls. There's a watch shop downtown. They said it's not something they normally would work on, but that he could handle. I was going to bring it tomorrow."

Her hands trembled a little as she took it from him. The weight of it had changed. She turned it over, pressing her thumb into the groove along its edge, then the hollow socket with the missing gnomon. It was sharp. Good. Something to hold onto. Something real.

"Was that wrong?" he asked. "I'm sorry."

She turned it in her palm. She didn't answer. But the words began to form. Words she had held back for so long. She might just let them escape this time. The coat was gone, thrown away without ceremony. If she hadn't already thrown it out, it might have changed how she reacted now. But that part of her was satisfied, for the time being. The sundial rested in her hands, heavier than it looked. And she was lighter for the first time in a long while. It was unsteady, like a fragile new shape in her hands that she would need to learn how to carry. Alone, perhaps. She buried what she was going to say; she didn't have the energy for it.

Chapter 20

Sable reentered the chamber at the citadel's core. She expected the air to be hostile. Instead, it was empty. A perfect, unbreathing vacuum waiting to be filled. Vesper followed, his sword still sheathed. He didn't know why he still carried it. A moment later, Sentinel emerged from the hall. He settled near the threshold. A quiet, gray witness to a confrontation he had no part in.

At the center of the room, the Edict hovered. Its mechanical frame was cast in cold, humming fluorescent light. Its gears turned in a rhythm of absolute certainty. Its features weren't monstrous, and there was no malice in its gears. It was entirely indifferent to her. Its evil lay in its argument, made manifest in metal and light. An argument that denied her right to be.

Its voice pressed. A direct impression of its truth pressed into thought.

Analysis: Anomaly Sable. Persistent deviation. Structural Integrity: Compromised. Outcome: Uncontained error.

The two remaining oracles, now perfectly synchronized, echoed the verdict. Their voices were a single, flat tone.

Outcome: Uncontained Error.

But something was missing. The third oracle left a void in the triad of what they represented. Without them, the cadence of the other two had grown inert.

Sable didn't raise her voice. She hadn't come here for a fight. She'd simply stepped forward, and the sterile air of the chamber recoiled from her. It was chilling. Like being unexpectedly seen by a hostile crowd. That familiar misalignment in her own skin.

"I'm not strange," she said. Her voice was shaky in the perfect silence. "I'm a variable that you forgot to account for."

The Edict's gears whirred, the sound accelerating slightly. The light of its glyphs sharpened as it parsed the statement. It was processing. Analyzing. Judging her composition not by the movement of her lines, but by how it fit the frame.

Analysis: Negative. All variables accounted for. Halt: Uncharted variable found. Processing: Error. Initiate: Erasure.

Vesper tensed, his hand instinctively going to the hilt of his sword. An uninvited reflex from a battle he no longer understood how to fight. Sable didn't even glance his way. Instead, she looked up at the Edict's unwavering gaze. And she invited it.

"No. I choose to hold it. To carry it because it's mine." Her words were not merely defiance, but a discovery. A sad, simple certainty. "Erasing something isn't a resolution. It's just... a deeper silence."

She reached into the pocket of her cloak. She touched fabric. It settled her.

The Edict acted first, re-initializing its protocol. It began to recontextualize.

The cold, obsidian floor shifted, then flickered. Then it resolved into polished and sterile white tiles. The low hum of the citadel sharpened into something high and anxious.

Beep. Beep. Beep.

The air grew thick. Something sharp against her throat. A smell that scraped. That seeped into fabric.

Logic Query: If grief is unbearable, then isn't erasure a mercy? You agreed to this logic. Return to it.

The pressure to comply was immense. Her posture began to fold inward. The name *Katherine* felt safer. She staggered, the breath catching in her throat.

Vesper cautiously took a half-step closer. This wasn't his fight. But he was here and that mattered. "Sable," he said. His voice was firm. "It's just stone and lies. The tile isn't here. The sound isn't real. You are."

His voice was an anchor. The scent of the observatory began to fade. And with it, something else surfaced. A lightning rod of anger pulsed in her bones. She didn't need to be reminded of her grief for it to be real. *The world had no fucking right to it.*

The Edict registered the failure. It began to recalibrate. As it did, the two remaining oracles advanced. They didn't do so separately. They had been joined in accord for so long. They still were. They moved forward, in concert. The empty space beside them was still hollow. But their movements mimicked the third oracle in a way that had to be intentional.

The first oracle, a current that had only known erasure, injected a single and pure memory into the chamber. The image of Penelope turning to face the light, her form unwritten. The thread was swept away by oblivion.

The Edict's processes stalled. It faltered, attempting to parse the new stream of data while simultaneously recalibrating its function towards Sable. It couldn't do both. And in that momentary lapse, the second oracle issued a new function into the space between them.

Logic: The Edict failed to protect a core component. The primary sector was erased by its own functions. Correction of external deviation is invalid until internal integrity can be restored. The pattern must yield.

A smile formed on Vesper's face. The pincer movement. The cold calculation of battlefield tactics bled into a space where certainty was the only battlefield that mattered. He was braced for a warzone. Instead, he was witnessing the Edict's function rendering itself inert.

The gears around them audibly hitched. The third oracle was gone. And the grief of it... the loss of a primary sector was more than a hairline fracture in the Edict's form. It was a crack that had already shown signs of rust forming.

A wound that couldn't be smoothed over by erasure. It was the result of it.

The white tile floor vanished. Shifted into something warmer. Wooden floorboards and an abrasive rug. Popcorn scattered throughout. Some under the bed. A piece touched an old shoebox. Dusty and forgotten.

The Edict was no longer a machine. It was a person. She sat on the floor, ankles crossed under her and bare knees jutting out to the sides. She held a folded letter in her hand. Two were already written and laid open before her.

Sable knelt nearby. It was her. Penelope. Or someone shaped like her. Her features were the same. But her face held a blank expression. A myth, cast into human form. Pressed into a shape small enough to walk side by side with someone who needed that kind of small strength. But also a spirit large enough to shatter rooms she hadn't been invited into.

The girl couldn't meet her eyes. She stared at her own hands instead. At the letter she held, folded. Not yet sealed. And that face offered no hint of explanation. No meaning as to why she held herself so still. Sable found nothing, and so she touched the first letter. Cold. Written by a machine that understood function more than care.

Sable,

Here's the address for the university post office. Here's my international calling card code. Don't lose it. I left the key to the storage unit taped under the sink. The books from last semester are in the blue bin. You can have the poetry ones, don't pretend you hate them. Pay my half of the phone bill with the cash in the top drawer. Call you when I settle.

That was it. No emotion. No apology. It was a set of instructions. Because when the world falls out from under you, the first thing you need is a task. A reason to get up and put your shoes on. A quest. She had given her a blueprint so she wouldn't drown in her feelings. It had grounded her in the here and now.

Sable reached for the second one. It singed her fingers.

Sable,

Look, I know this sucks. I know you're probably freaking out. But this is for me. I have to do this for me. I can't spend my whole life making sure you're okay. I can't be your anchor if I'm drowning, too. So be mad. I don't care. I'm going.

It was brutal. And it was mostly a lie. Of course she cared. But Sable... she now understood why she had written it. Sable had this quiet way of absorbing blame. Of turning everything inward and until it became her fault. Penelope couldn't let her do that. She had to give her somewhere to put the anger. She had to give her an antagonist. Better she be furious with the selfish girl in that letter than with the memory of her best friend. She made a good alibi.

Only, Penelope hadn't realized what Sable would do with it. She didn't know that the third letter would be cast into the fire. The letter that mattered. The one that would stop her from turning the friend into a myth. Of internalizing the loss and building a life around that emptiness.

Sable reached for the third letter. The one still folded. She stopped an inch away from touching it, then let her hand drop to her side. The girl's eyes finally drifted up to her.

Sable searched the face for her friend. That failed. The features were only a reflection. A memory from college. Penelope hunched over a table, writing something for her anthropology class. Sable's back to her. Sketching something she couldn't recall now.

A sigh behind her as Penelope's pen ran out of ink. Sable had reached down, picked up a pencil and handed it to her. It was a B3. Not for writing. But good enough for the moment. Penelope hadn't said a word. They just continued. Because they had this understanding that sometimes the silence mattered.

Sable forced her eyes upward. "You're not her, are you?" she said.

The girl wearing Penelope's face turned. It met her gaze. Cold. Hollow. An uncanny recreation of someone that mattered deeply. A sick joke played against someone who was desperate.

"Aren't you going to read it?" It asked. And there it was. A desperation in the girl's voice.

Sable wasn't here to defeat the Edict, because it would never be defeated. It could only be made irrelevant.

"I've read it before. I don't need to read it again." She swallowed. "You don't get to tell my story, live my life, or tell me how to perform. You're not her, and you never were. That might be my fault, but I won't let it shape what happens next."

And with that, the room shifted. The cold and humming obsidian walls and floor returned. The gears above her still twisted.

Sable let out a slow breath. For once, the Edict saw her as she was. And it didn't understand.

The Edict's relentless, grinding rhythm softened. It didn't stop, but the aggressive, interrogating edge had gone. The gears slowed. A near-silent, observational rotation. The piercing diagnostic light at its core dimmed. It was replaced by a steady, neutral glow. The shift from a weapon to a mirror.

The Edict wasn't trying to correct her anymore. It was trying to understand. It couldn't. But it was trying.

"You don't believe me," she said. "I don't need you to. It might be enough, if I do."

Now it was Sable who studied her own hands. They were just hands. No blurring. Nothing unusual about them. They could have been anybody's. But they were hers. Still in a crouch, she lowered herself further and sat the way the girl in the vision had. Scuffed knees to the world. Her hands met the cool touch of the floor. It was solid. It was real. Where the letters had laid before her, now there was only dust. It didn't ache. It was space.

Behind her, Vesper took a hesitant step closer. His face bore something of awe and confusion. His sword, still at his side, was just an empty weight. A pointless artifact. It was the first time he wasn't actually trying to solve her. He stopped analyzing and simply saw who she was. Who she was becoming.

"Sable?" he whispered. A question. A confirmation.

She turned to him and her lips quirked into an awkward smile. Tired. Impossibly small. The smile of someone who had just won a war by surrendering the right piece of herself.

"Come on," she said. "Let's go home."

The word home hung in the air. A concept more complex and fractured than the Edict.

They walked toward the threshold. Sentinel, who had been a silent, gray statue, rose to meet them. There was no triumph in his posture. He was simply done. The patter of his feet fell into step behind them. The limp still present. A rhythm to accompany their own.

The Edict remained behind them. It hummed its quiet, endless loop of observation. Mirrored surfaces shimmered. They no longer reflected her. They showed possibilities. The gears would likely spin for eternity. But it no longer mattered. Its gaze was fixed on a memory that it couldn't solve. It left the rest of the world unsupervised. Dangerous.

The Loom hadn't healed. Its scars remained. More of them began to appear, glimpsed through threads of embroidery not wound tight enough to hide them fully. But the relentless pressure to correct was left out of focus. Still there, but lessened. Her world was now free to be messy. To be wrong. To be overwhelming in all the worst ways. And all the best ways.

Vesper's hand found hers; it carried the same uncertainty. A needle searching for a thread needing to be stitched. "Are you still here?" he asked.

She didn't tighten her grip. But she didn't pull away, either. The contact was so distant, as if filtered through layers of fabric. The veil around them rippled at the answer she might give. Would it be truthful, or for her or for him? He had no right to ask it, but he had. And now she reeled.

Am I still here?

Part Four

Chapter 21

THE CLOCK TICKED, BUT without urgency. Light stretched long across the counter, slanting gold across the rim of the sink. August's plans for the morning were already in motion. A trip to the farmers market, lunch at their usual spot. The air held a kind of expectancy, like the day had already decided how it wanted to unfold.

Sable stood in the kitchen, hands wrapped around a warm mug. The tile sent a sharp chill up through her heels. Her knees. A change. The faintly bitter scent of coffee clung to the air around her.

August entered, his steps casual, unfussed. The kind that arrived without needing to be heard. He stood in the doorway, one hand on the frame, watching her without interruption. The hesitation between them stayed awkward, present, stitched into their routine like anything else.

"You've been quiet lately," he said. He had said this before. Time and time again. This time, his words seemed to leave his mouth before he was ready to speak them.

She didn't answer at first. The mug in her hands held its heat, steam unwinding in thin, uncertain spirals. Her eyes flicked up to him just once. She opened her mouth, ready to say the wrong thing and mean it.

The phone buzzed. Priya's name lit the screen. Sable's eyes flicked toward the phone, focus already beginning to loosen. She held herself there. It was an effort. August didn't say anything else, but he waited. He could have walked away, probably should have, but he didn't. He waited, and the pause held.

"I know," she said eventually, her voice low and controlled. Her thumb swiped a message away. "I'm trying to figure it out."

She glanced up again. Their eyes met for a beat longer than they usually held.

"I'm not okay," she added. Priya's words from the other day surfaced, and she continued, "But I'm not lost either. I'm still here, you know."

August nodded once, measured. No surprise. No urgency. The kind of nod that accepted what was offered and knew not to ask for more. The phone buzzed again. This time she let it. A distant sound, meant for another version of her. August stepped back, just enough to mark the distance. His movement aligned with the trajectory of their relationship. She didn't follow or retreat. She remained where she stood.

Later, when the rustle and calamity had settled and the last heat had left her mug, August picked up his keys and his coat. It was time for them to go.

She opened the bedroom closet. The air bit at her hands, unexpected and sharp. Then, her fingers brushed fabric she didn't expect, startling her. Her hand found the old coat as if by instinct. Wool, worn thin at the elbows. The color had faded where the shoulders had weathered sun and rain. The lining held the shape of her arms. Familiar in the way some memories are, persistent.

Seeing it here, after all this time, was to see it for what it was. Rundown. Haggard. The loose threads and frayed edges that had grounded her, that gave her the power to become invisible when she needed to be, were barely holding together. But still, he had folded it with care. Set aside like something meant to return. He hadn't thrown it out. He must have put it away when he bought her new one.

Her thumb caught on a frayed thread at the cuff. She knew this coat; she had disappeared inside it on long walks. She had curled beneath its heft on afternoons when the world was far away. It had been armor. A cloak that drifted and clung while walking through the faultline. It had been home. She could just sink into it once again.

The air around her trembled. And she did, too. Touching it. She was already drifting through a current toward oblivion. She could put it on. Don the cloak. Assume the role she had lived in for so long.

Behind her, August stood in the hallway. He said nothing, but his eyes pierced her. Witnessing. Or maybe it was Vesper's eyes. She didn't turn to check.

Instead, she let go. Her hand drifted past the coat, then brushed a different fabric, one buried beneath seasons. The material was rust-colored. Muted, warm. It resisted her pull, creaking as she lifted it, reluctant and stiff with disuse. Like it remembered how long it had been forgotten.

She took it anyway, pulled it close, let it reshape around her. The lining was cold against her skin, its shape heavier than she remembered. It didn't feel like hers, but it didn't belong to anyone else. Maybe she didn't either. She adjusted the collar, the fabric brushing her jaw, then she let it settle.

Her reflection confronted her in the hall mirror as she passed it. She startled at the expression. A woman on the verge of saying something reckless.

The apartment hadn't changed. The shadows fell in their same angles, and the warmth gathered at corners she didn't visit. It bore the faint trace of morning toast and dusty corridors. But she was different. No, not different. *Forming.*

From where August watched her, the floor was split. A line of light ran across the wood floor between them. Her phone buzzed again. *Priya.* She reached for it, thumb hovering over the screen, then paused. She wasn't certain where today would lead. But her skin wasn't asking her to vanish. *Maybe, that's enough.*

Her thumb swiped. She lifted the phone to her ear, the line connecting with a soft click.

"Sable?" Priya's voice came through.

Sable stood there in the quiet of her silent apartment. One version of herself waited for the right words. Another might speak before those words were fully understood. The line remained open, waiting for her choice.

Chapter 22

Morning light slid through the curtains, pooling in thin streaks across the counter. The low hum of distant traffic and the rhythm of birdsong filtered in through the open window. It was background noise to a morning that asked nothing of her. Sable sat at the table sketching with charcoal, a warm mug nearby. The warmth didn't reach far. On the windowsill, the sundial caught the light. The bronze gleamed along its broken edge.

A detail surfaced. A broken field, shattered stone spires jutting up from crystalline floors. The Loom redrawing itself along the horizon. The air moved differently now, remembering a rhythm it had forgotten.

Sable paused at the threshold of what had once been a great sanctuary. She pressed her palm to blackened and fragmented stone. The surface was cool and gritty, and left her palm stained. Vesper's footsteps crunched softly behind her. He walked like a man learning to tiptoe around an injury. What passed between them was a breach learning to reshape itself into an understanding. How could she ever begin again?

The two remaining oracles approached. Their faces, still featureless, somehow revealed something that looked like curiosity. And something more.

The second oracle tangled their stance, the graceless effort of a newborn deer learning to walk. The oracles had never allowed themselves to move out of sync with each other. They looked unmoved in their resolve, but no longer confident. And when the second oracle finally spoke, their words had the old sharpness, but it was as if the blade had dulled.

"I knew they were going to defect," they said, inclining their shoulder towards the first oracle. "I could see it. After the third, I realized... I would soon be alone. Angry and unsure why."

They took in a deep breath. For the first time? "That shouldn't have mattered, but it did; I didn't want to be alone. But we thought necessity meant control. We diverged, yes. But still the compulsion to correct remains. Why do I still need to?"

The words hung between them. A diagnosis disguised as a verdict. Vesper glanced between the three of them. He didn't speak. Good. It meant he might be learning when not to.

The second oracle continued. "Perfect was... a projection. I see it now. I once held a name, though it won't form. I may never get it back." Their cadence was shaped by a clarity that had once cut through all doubt. It threatened to do so again. "My designation has stepped aside, and yet

I remember it. Why do I remember that, and not who I was?"

The phone buzzed against the counter. Her fingers hovered over the screen, then she tapped the button to answer.

"Sorry, Penelope, I've just…"

She cut her off. "Hey," Penelope said, easy and bright. "I was thinking about that road trip. Do you remember?"

Sable pulled herself back into the world she knew. The one where memories hurt differently, and fears didn't leave because she named them. "The camping trip? Not really."

"You remember how you nearly got us kicked out of the store for narrating everything like a wildlife special?"

Sable blinked, the memory arriving. "Oh god. 'Observe the urban cryptid in her natural habitat, hoarding timepieces she doesn't understand.'"

They both laughed. Sable's shoulders shook.

"Yeah. You couldn't stop talking about that sundial. You said it felt important, like you had to have it. Do you remember how much you needed it?"

Sable closed her eyes. The store reassembled before her in fragments. Dust curling through a shaft of light, shelves crowded with forgotten things. Penelope's shoulder brushed hers. Quick. Unremarkable.

The air smelled of old paper and worn brass, and the anis oil Penelope always used when she twisted her hair up. Her yiayia made it, she once told Sable, steeped for three days in a jar wrapped with red string and prayers she never translated. She called it *yiatrikó* and simply said it was a family thing. Sable had remembered that scent, and even after Penelope left she would think of her every time she saw the word anise.

Her hand had brushed the sundial's curve. It tipped sideways, clattering off the shelf, loud enough to make them both flinch. Penelope caught it before it fell to the floor, but just barely. She handed it to Sable. Then Sable had closed her fingers around it, and was solid. Something that was meant to be there. Like she was meant to hold it.

"I think I remember," she said. "It broke on the way home."

"Yeah," Penelope said. "The piece that casts the shadow. You looked everywhere. It really got to you. But you said something that I've never forgotten, even when it took me far away to come back to it. Do you remember what it was?"

Sable had walked over to the window, as if drawn. She reached down and traced the edge of the sundial. "No. It... it's like a dream. That day's somewhere under the surface now. Like it drifted too far downriver to find again."

"You said, 'It doesn't have to be perfect. It just has to be mine.'"

Sable pressed her thumb to the flaw on the sundial's surface. "I forgot," she said. "But I think I've been carrying it all along."

"I know," Penelope said. Her next words barely rose above a breath. "Yeah, you've been carrying that broken thing around like a religious relic, haven't you? Are you still doing that?"

A sharp intake of breath on Sable's end. A silence so loud it had a texture.

"It's a convenient habit, forgetting the things that force you to make a decision," Penelope continued, her voice clinical now. "But you can't keep staring at the empty space forever, waiting for the shadow to tell you what time it is."

Another silence. Then, softer, but still firm. "The offer to actually talk about it is on the table, Sable. It's your move."

Sable didn't answer right away. Her thumb traced the arc of the missing gnomon again. "You," Sable began, uncertain how the sentence would finish. "You left. And..."

"And I trusted you to put yourself back together." Penelope finished the sentence for her.

A tear began to fall. The first in ages. She clutched the sundial. "I shouldn't have had to."

Penelope didn't answer. Maybe she couldn't. Maybe she didn't know what to say. But they stayed in silence for a long time, only listening to each others breaths over the line. Sable wanted to go on. She'd had this conversation a thousand times before in her head. But now, nothing else would come. And she didn't know if she wanted it to. She wanted to tell her about what happened. All of it. To open the shoebox and lay it all bare before her. But that box was sealed with filament and rage. And she didn't want to be angry. She only wanted to be understood.

And Penelope, she never broke that silence. She waited. And soon, Sable realized that Penelope never would. They'd stay on this line together for an hour in silence if necessary, because she was waiting. Because she knew that Sable had more to say. She knew that if she spoke now, she'd shape that choice and shape those words. Penelope had the wisdom, the beautiful and horrible wisdom, to let Sable decide what shape they took.

And so, she went on. "You would have cried when you saw his face. You would have said he was the most beautiful thing you've ever seen."

The tears fell now. Not all at once. Oblivion leaned in, and she leaned against it, straining to claim the space she stood in. It mattered.

Penelope didn't push. She didn't ask for more than that. The silence was its own understanding. Eventually, the conversation drifted, wandering here and there. It never truly finished. There was no goodbye. There didn't need to be.

After the call, Sable sat the phone down. Her fingers rested on the sundial, her mind distant. The words echoed back to her. *It doesn't have to be perfect. It just has to be mine.*

The missing piece was gone. The part that gave it meaning, the part that measured her hours and days in moments that made life worth it. It didn't just cast a shadow. It held a shape. It was gone. But she remained.

Outside, a car door shut louder than it should have. The sound was distant, irrelevant. She stayed where she was, as if movement might undo something that had finally settled.

She ran her fingers through her hair absently. The weight stayed. She moved slowly, hoping the day wouldn't crack under her feet. It didn't. It held. But something underneath had shifted.

At work, something moved with her. It lingered in the frayed edge of her chair, the scuffed corner of her desk. In the half-second pauses before nods from colleagues who sensed the difference without naming it. She moved through it all deliberately, as if navigating a room she once knew by heart and no longer trusted in the dark.

She attended a meeting. There, sunlight sliced across the table. Paper rustled. Voices murmured. She read through the agenda. Her name. *Katherine.* Her fingers paused on it.

Later, she stepped into a café. Espresso and conversation saturated the space, forming its own weather system, humming low beneath the clatter of cups. Near the counter, a young woman hunched over a sketchpad, pencil moving in loose, searching arcs.

"That's lovely," Sable said, her voice louder than she meant it to be.

The woman looked up, startled, then smiled. "Thanks. I didn't even realize anyone was watching."

Had she been watching? Something in the girl's eyes said this wasn't an intrusion. Tentatively, Sable stepped closer, gently leaning in. "It's... peaceful."

"I've been trying to catch a feeling. You ever get that? Like something barely out of frame, and if you stop moving long enough, maybe you'll see it."

Sable's gaze dropped to the sketch. A field rendered in graphite smudge, a tree tilting against a wind that was suggested in the slant of its trunk. Shadows stretched beneath it, three of them, almost parallel, but not quite. They didn't match the light. Or each other.

"The shadows... They feel heavier than the tree. Do you ever draw something just to see the shape of its shadow?" she asked, almost to herself.

The woman blinked. Her pencil stilled. Then she smiled, slow. The kind that only comes after recognition.

"Yeah," she said. "That's exactly it. Because sometimes what you're trying to see is already on the page."

Sable tilted her head, studying the sketch. "It's hard to tell if it's finished."

"Finished? What's that?" The woman laughed. "But I think I know where it wants to go."

A question began to form, but she swallowed it before it could escape. The woman looked down, as if the page might have changed on its own.

"You draw?" she asked without looking up.

"Sometimes," Sable said. "It helps; if I can lay my whole world down on canvas, it makes it all start to fit. All the characters. When I'm trying to remember something that doesn't want to be remembered."

The woman didn't press. They didn't even close the conversation.

Sable took her coffee to a corner table, and they didn't speak again, although they were only a few feet away from each other. The cup held warmth the way a stone holds sun, faint, already fading. She stared at the wall for a long time. Light shifted across it like something passing through, unseen.

Vesper and the anomaly walked now, just the two of them. He turned to her as they drew near an obelisk of gray, unadorned rock. It was solid. It looked ancient. As they shifted around it, they saw Sentinel resting nearby. He sat on his haunches, staring up at it. His body was failing. He endured, but with great effort.

"This began with you," Vesper said. The words were full of reverence, and he placed his hand on the monument. "Your sacrifice changed everything. We'll remember it."

Sentinel turned his head to them both. His gaze was heavy with the weight of eons. After seeing them, he turned his dull yellow eyes back to the monument.

"Don't mistake my decision for peace," he said. His voice was a low growl that vibrated through stone. Each word sounded strained. "I gave what I had because none of you ever stopped to wonder what I might need. Not once."

He let the words hang there. Then he turned his head to regard them. "Sable, I held your memory so that you didn't have to. And Vesper, I kept your stillness so that you could break." He exhaled, and it sounded final. "You call that sacrifice? I call it theft."

Vesper flinched, his head lowering. Sable's hands fidgeted at her sides.

Sentinel's gaze swept back to the monument, then toward the path they had walked. Up to the hollow spire. "And now you want to archive me. You stand here admiring a monument, but all I see is one of the Edict's alcoves. A polished, perfect, empty space waiting for my story to be sanitized and filed away. Something to make you feel better about the cost."

He pushed himself to his feet, his knees buckling slightly before holding. He turned his body to face them fully. "You want to make a thread out of what I bleed for? No. You don't have the right to it."

His voice dropped. No longer a growl, but quiet. Almost human in its sharpness. "Don't grieve me. Carry what I gave, and carry what you took. And if they ever ask who paid for your wholeness, tell them my name. And tell them how it wasn't yours to use."

Then he turned and walked away. His limp was steady and rhythmic. An indictment of the very ground he walked on. He left no blessing behind, only a terrible clarity.

On the way home, she watched her reflection on the train glass. It blurred, shifting with the movement under her. The artist's words echoed. *Trying to catch a feeling*. Sable had spent a lifetime trying to do the opposite. To let her feelings pass through without being caught.

An old memory surfaced, unbidden, with the clatter of the tracks. The atmosphere of Penelope's apartment as a kid. Coats piled onto a single hook. Crocheted blankets draped over the arms of the couch. It had been a sea of textures and senses. The uneven tick of the kitchen clock, her mother's footsteps pacing, the aroma of olive oil and garlic from the kitchen, and the low, constant hum of a high-voltage wire that was Penelope's father. He was a big man, his laugh sounding like rocks in a tumbler. He filled the space he was in. Except when he didn't.

Sable remembered being there one afternoon, watching Penelope argue fiercely about philosophy, gesturing with a piece of toast, loud and brilliant. And then the phone rang. Penelope's father answered, and his face went tight. An official call. Immigration, maybe. Or the bank.

And Sable had watched him. This man who filled the world, shrank. He stood straighter, his voice became smaller, more polite. More correct. He became accommodating. He held the phone like it was a live grenade.

Penelope, the warrior, went utterly silent; she didn't move. She just watched her father, her shoulders tensed, her jaw set. A silent, terrified sentinel. The same way she stood when a teacher had circled her name on the board.

Now, sitting here on the train, the pattern began to settle. The need for Penelope to be larger than life, and the moments when she made herself small. Her silence was a spire built around his vulnerability. So was her fire.

Sable had always seen her friend as two people. The unstoppable force and the girl who sometimes froze. But they weren't two people. They were one person, doing whatever it took. Whether sometimes abrasive or sometimes making herself invisible, it was about choosing the right weapon for the right war.

I saw you, Sable thought, her own reflection looking back at her from the darkened glass. I saw both of you.

She walked home as the sky tilted toward dusk. She held the streets at a distance, like scenery behind glass. Without urgency. She carried the cardboard mug in her hand, barely noticing how the warmth had become weight. It pressed inward, instead of down.

At the apartment, the hallway light flickered once as she unlocked the door. August looked up from the couch when she stepped in. He didn't speak right away. He met her eyes, waiting. He looked relieved.

She leaned down, kissed him. Soft. Automatic. It didn't anchor either of them.

Then she stepped past him, deeper into the living room. The window was cracked open, letting in a faint breath of the city. Traffic hummed somewhere below, a low rhythm she couldn't quite sync with. She sat the coffee down on the table, stood beside it. The silence didn't press; it settled, like dust on forgotten furniture.

Her eyes drifted to the edge of the couch. Her hand twitched, almost reached underneath, as if something might be there. A receipt. A monument. A scrap of cloth. She didn't know.

She didn't move. Whatever it was, she knew that it wasn't here. The gnomon had broken somewhere else. Lost far away. Not coming back.

Chapter 23

THE MEETING ROOM REVERBERATED with low conversation, chairs shifting, the sharp clink of ceramic on ceramic from coffee cups left too close to elbows. Sunlight filtered through the blinds. Steady. Angled in sharp stripes across the long table. Sable sat, her fingertips resting on the wood, tracing a familiar groove on its edge. She adjusted her glasses, automatic. Her gaze remained watchful and unreadable.

Dr. Harlan was guiding the group through the upcoming audit prep timeline. She listened. Each exchange passed cleanly from speaker to speaker, her thoughts registering every pivot, every dismissal. When it was her turn, she spoke clearly, her voice even, deliberate. The room moved on.

No questions. No pause. Just a faint nod before someone changed the subject. Her hand stilled. She kept her gaze low. The words had left and then vanished, absorbed by the surface of the table.

A moment later, someone echoed her words, nearly identical phrasing. It landed. She watched the eyes focus their attention, a murmur of acknowledgment, the slow lift of a few heads. Someone smiled, as if the idea had just arrived.

Sable's thumb pressed into the wood. She reoriented, shoulders loose. Lungs steadying.

"Actually," she said, louder than she expected, "that was the idea I proposed a few moments ago."

The silence that followed was a mixture of both surprise and embarrassment. Hers included. Penelope had once told her something. *You don't need to sound polished. You just need to sound like you meant it.*

She hadn't sounded polished. But she had meant it. Her throat burned anyway.

Dr. Harlan looked up, met her eyes. "You're right, Sable," he said. "Let's explore that further."

She nodded. Her fingers let go of the table. When conversation resumed, its pacing had turned. The room bent slightly. The voices were softer, the pattern altered.

The commute home stretched, windows streaked. Glass, motion, dusk layered over itself. Sable's reflection floated there, hovering just off-center. She didn't blink it away. Didn't correct it. Let it stay.

The hearth was meant to be a place of convergence. Stone walls curved inward, etched with threads of memory. Some were barely lit, others had been reduced to ash.

A flame hovered in the center, suspended without fuel. Vesper knelt beside the flame, the warmth stopping about a foot from the stone. It left his back cold, despite the warmth near his hands. He laid down tokens that were important to him. A broken watch. A small piece of fabric, frayed at its edges. And a child's mask, worn smooth.

He arranged them carefully; off-center, crooked, close enough. The oracles would arrive soon. They were being returned. Guardians of the Loom. She watched from the room's edges. She didn't speak, choosing to wait. She needed to know if he would catch himself before making the obvious mistake.

When Sable stepped into the apartment, the light had already begun to fade. The space was dim, a hush that hadn't been disturbed, only waiting.

August looked up from across the room, caught mid-step, her unfinished painting in his hands. One foot slightly turned, elbow bent, the canvas suspended awkwardly between movement and retreat.

"August," she said. Her voice didn't rise. She stepped forward, grasping the canvas tightly along the edge. He didn't move at first, then his eyes met hers.

"Oh, sorry. I thought I'd help clean up."

She shook her head. "I'd like to decide what stays out. Don't touch my things."

She could have left it at that. But something deep stirred. Something ancient. Something dangerous, and reckless, and buried for far too long.

"If I didn't want it there, don't you think I would have put it away a long time ago?" She tried to keep her voice low, but that only made it rise and fall, unsteady and sharp. "Stop trying to help. I don't need you to fix everything. Not everything that looks out of place, actually is. Sometimes..."

Her voice caught. She might cry or scream. Or break something. "Sometimes, I need something to stay wrong. It just... sometimes it matters. And I don't need people to tell me how it could be better."

His hands released the canvas. They held themselves open for a while, even after releasing. He was letting go of something else. A small nod of his head, more gesture than agreement.

She sat the painting against the wall, where it was. The canvas met the floor with a dull sound. Final. It stayed there, leaning slightly, catching what light was left. Unfinished streaks of color clung to the canvas like a life in motion.

"I don't remember this," the first oracle intoned. Their voice still rippled and reverberated, but there was a touch more humanity to its cadence. "This memory isn't mine."

The second oracle approached the thread, then sifted through the ashes below it with their foot. They bent down, picked something up from it. Then discarded it into the flame. "You think I chose silence? I didn't and I won't pretend that I did."

Vesper ran a hand through his hair. An old gesture he made when he was weighing what to say. He sat down by the hearth. "I just want things to get back to how they were," he said, reluctantly.

"Is... is that what you think this is?" Sable hadn't addressed him until now; it wasn't fire or anger in her eyes, but a painful recognition. He was still trying to frame things from his perspective.

He didn't answer her. But then the second oracle touched a thread. "This one," they said. "The third oracle refused to name this one. They said it wasn't anybody else's to name." Then they flicked the thread. It thrummed, violet and green waves extending from it. Then they pinched it, broke it free from where it was attached and let the flame have it.

Then they left, and Sable followed. Vesper sat, alone, staring at the child's mask in the ash. He picked it up. An urge washed over him. To put it back on. To feel how well it lined up with the scar on his jaw. How it properly framed him. How it made him reliable, functional, a valued member of the community. He had laid bare everything that mattered, and the oracles didn't understand. They couldn't. Because maybe what he remembered was only the shadow of what was actually true.

He sat the mask back down. Not in the flame, just resting in the ash. He placed it there, almost as if he might change his mind later. "Not everything is mine to protect," he said. "Not everything is mine to hold." And then he followed the others and left the hearth to gather ash and dust.

The room held steady as the golden light dimmed. Shadows pooled into corners, as if witnessing the day come to a close.

She crossed to the window. The sundial sat on the sill, lit by the last narrow brush of dusk. She could pick it up and smash it against the wall. Her fingers started to reach. A pause. Her hand lowered and she stood there and let the first tears since her call with Penelope run down her cheeks.

August approached later, stopping a half-step behind her, then placed a hand on her shoulder. He leaned forward, pressed a kiss to her damp cheek. She leaned into it. He stepped back, shifted slightly. His lips risked the formation of words. Words he bit back before turning toward the kitchen instead. His footsteps made no sound, but the air stirred in his absence.

Sable lowered herself into the chair by the window. The blanket remained folded on the couch, its pattern unreadable in the fading light. A mug from the morning sat on the table, now cold, half-full.

She looked around. Nothing had moved. Nothing was rearranged. But something had returned. She said nothing. And she didn't vanish. And that meant something. It meant that the dread she had been carrying was still there. Still threatening to burst forward. That it might arrive in a rage, and she didn't know what shape it might take tomorrow. She was capable of anything now, and that was a terrible idea to have when she didn't quite know what she wanted.

Chapter 24

THE GLADES DIDN'T WELCOME him back. The land barely recognized him.

Sentinel moved alone beneath a canopy of shifting trees, his shape stretched thin. The forest watched him pass through. Forgotten. No title accompanied his return. No summons. No purpose. The air, which once held breath and memory in careful suspension, now pulsed with a low, feverish restlessness.

Vines like arteries, coiled through the canopy. They threaded themselves into branches that hadn't been there before. Petals of unnamed flowers shuddered open and shut in a spastic rhythm. In the undergrowth, the constant, dry rustle of unseen things rose to meet him. The skittering of insects. The whisper of decaying leaves. Roots crawled beneath the soil like nerves searching for signal.

The mist, once a quiet veil, now clung to him. It was a damp, abrasive static that smelled of wet soil and the sharp, metallic tang of decay and new growth clashing. It grated against his flanks. His feline form drifted forward, stretched thinner than he had been last time he was here. The ground yielded like feverish skin, soft and porous.

A branch, slick with moss, scraped across his shoulder and a violent shudder wracked his nerves. He lunged at the empty air beside it, a guttural snarl tearing from his throat as his claws sliced through nothing. He landed, panting, every muscle coiled for a fight against a foe that was only a memory of pressure. The ghost-sensation of the veil's touch was a static charge on his hide.

The branch that had touched him withdrew with a slow, indifferent curl. It offered no apology.

Trees he once passed without notice were now swollen like bruised tissue, their trunks split and knotted where order had failed. Others had curled inward, leafless. Their bark peeled back in thin ribbons like sunburnt skin. Layer upon layer of moss, a vibrant and aggressive green, grew in thick patches where memory had once held form. A scar that wouldn't fade.

He reached the grove. Once, a shrine had been rooted here, swallowed beneath an overturned tree. Now the roots had thickened, swollen and twisted together like a dense knot of scar tissue. The carving was gone. Erased. Or, perhaps rewritten into the soil so many times that it had forgotten what it once meant.

Sentinel lowered himself onto his haunches and listened; he held his breath. From deep within the tangled roots, a sound rose. A high, brief laugh. It snagged in the air like a thread on a thorn. Sable's laugh, perhaps. Or a memory shaped like her. It was too distant to hold. Too sharp to dismiss.

The sound didn't come again. In its place, the forest seemed to draw a single, collective breath. The sound of a thousand leaves rustling in unison, holding it in, unsure how to let it go again.

His gaze remained on the knot of roots. "This body was never meant to grow without an anchor to keep it true," he said aloud. He diagnosed the wound, then became disgusted at the sight of it. "This place doesn't need me anymore." The words were foreign on his tongue and the roots did not respond.

He turned toward the pool that once held clarity. The water hesitated. It used to draw coherence from what was carried into it. Echoing truth back to those who stepped near. Now it was milky at the edges, distorted. A cataract forming over a vast, unblinking eye.

Sentinel circled it once, his paws silent on the damp moss. When he stopped at the edge, his reflection wavered, refusing to cohere. No longer a panther. It was something angular, longer. A flicker of a form stretched and pulled by time. A ghost haunting the forest's clouded vision.

He crouched, the dampness of the moss seeping into the pads of his paws. He pressed one paw to the ground, pushing it deep into the moss. A strain ran through his shoulder. An effort he hadn't exerted in eons. Glyphs surfaced in the soil, reluctant and faint.

Perform. Witness. Guard. Break.

They flickered, their glow weak. The pull in his marrow. A deep, resonating tone meant for the old, ordered world. The language of containment. The grammar of a role placed upon him long before he knew how to refuse it. The glyphs dimmed, sputtering out like dying nerves. The soil rejected them, scouring them away until only the blackened, inert mud remained. The pool's surface recoiled, shuddering as if from a bad memory or a ghostly chill.

Brief, broken images pulsed from the water's milky surface. A branch twisting into a knot. A name caught in a throat, unspoken. A structure collapsing into a silent plume of ash.

He rose too quickly. A jolt of something like fear, or perhaps just surprise, making his muscles bunch. Behind him, a branch lashed out with the speed of a striking snake. It hit a nearby stone, shattering it. The sound was a sharp crack that echoed unnaturally in the grove. Shards of rock and torn bark rained down. If it had been aimed at him, he wouldn't have moved in time. He was slow and the forest knew it.

"It never listened." The truth weighed on him, a cold sediment in his gut. "I was only ever its echo."

In a tree above, a crow cawed once. A harsh, grating sound. Then it launched itself into the air, wings beating a frantic retreat. He looked one last time into the pool. It showed him nothing. Only the clouded, shifting light. He turned from its unseeing eye and walked on. The ground refused to offer any firmness beneath his paws.

He saw a tree that hadn't been there before. It stood crooked at the forest's edge, rooted in soil that sagged. Ground that had never decided what it was meant to hold. Its trunk wasn't bark, but a cancerous knot of thread, light, and shadow. It twisted together too tightly. The strands pulled against one another, fraying where they met. It looked less grown than forced into place. As if something had tried to weave a pattern but lost the structure along the way.

Sentinel approached, his posture low. His hackles rose; every instinct screamed that this was wrong. The air around the tree grew unnaturally frosty. A low-frequency thrum began to vibrate through the soil, setting his teeth on edge. The tree pulsed with a sick, arrhythmic beat. Like a diseased heart caught between worlds.

He crouched. At its base, the threads knotted into a dense core. It looked like scar tissue. And from the center of that knot, a sound. Faint, rapid tapping. Like bone against ceramic. It didn't echo. It simply was.

He froze. The tapping stopped. The silence that followed was a vacuum, pulling at his eardrums. Beneath the roots, something shifted. Restless. Withheld. He reached a hesitant paw toward the knot.

It throbbed once, violently. A sharp crack split the air as the threads snapped backward, recoiling from his touch in an involuntary spasm.

Sentinel withdrew his paw. His body forced him back a step to match the movement. He didn't try again. The tree shuddered, and its presence seemed to press outward. He didn't ask why; he already knew the forest wouldn't answer.

But a low growl rumbled in his chest, a sound of pure contempt. "You tried to weave a god," he said. His gaze fixed on the knot. "And all you made was a cage." He turned away and left the sickened tree behind.

He walked until the trees gave way to thinning soil and the sky began to fracture in its familiar way. The Glade's boundary was a slow, cellular decay. An unraveling of nature into the harshness of the faultline. Roots grew sparse, tapering into the emptiness of dead nerves. Above, the sky bent without shape. Clouds twisting at impossible angles. A cascade of light moving without a source. The wind circled, carrying only the feeling of motion, but without its conviction.

Sentinel stood there. At the threshold of the fault-line. The ground beneath his paws thinned to a translucent membrane. More memory than substance. A wave of vertigo washed over him. Like he might fall through the present into the layers of the past he saw below. Earlier forests, layered like tissue under a microscope. One bore the shrine. Another showed the clear pool. Another showed nothing at all. Only barren soil.

In one layer, a version of himself stared back. Solid, radiant, certain. A version of him that might have belonged. That version was gone, if it had ever truly existed. That role, performed so often, had mistaken itself for real. His reflection in the membrane flickered. Panther. Shadow. Something else. A shape without edges. A presence unmoored from form.

This was what they saw. Panther. Guardian. Stillness incarnate. That wasn't his truth. Just the one they had kept. He met the gaze of his own glorified memory, and a wave of profound, bitter anger surged through him. For what he had lost. But also for what had been demanded of him. "Don't you have a performance to attend to?" he snarled at the reflection.

Then her. *Sable*. In one of the older forests. And with her, Penelope. Before Sable had turned her into a myth. They were whole and already moving forward. And then they diverged. When he looked at one, he couldn't see the other. Each of their backs were to him. He looked to Sable. She had progressed beyond the need for what he had once offered. What she had taken. What they had all taken. He hadn't been left behind at all.

His muscles let go. The tension he had carried in his shoulders, the constant readiness to intervene, it all simply dissolved. He let go of all of it. He had simply stayed too long.

"Tell them my name," he had said. The memory of the words were a stranger's. Heavy and demanding in his own throat. Here, even that felt like another performance. They weren't owed it.

He sat, the unstable ground holding his weight without complaint. The wind that moved through the unraveling world was no longer a judgement. Just an indifferent breath. Part of a lung system that no longer required his input. He closed his eyes and the forest didn't answer. But it didn't reject him, either. He remained. Another cell in a body that was learning to live with its scars.

He had carried the name Sentinel like a stone. And it brought a sense of pride, but also a resistance to the role. It was a clean inheritance. Now, the forest grew quiet and offered no direction. Who had placed that stone before him? Who gave him this name?

He couldn't remember choosing it. Only wearing it. Only being placed. An exhausted truth settling into his bones. He had been painted on the canvas because his presence balanced the composition. A shadow to give their colors depth. He had never asked to be seen. This wasn't his story to shape. He was only a stillness, a monument formed not out of stone, but out of need. Placed to make their movement legible.

Sable's hand trembled slightly as she wiped away the last bits of charcoal dust from the page, then she tore it from the book. The sound was both terrifying and deeply satisfying. She held it up, looking at his eyes. Cool, tired. They didn't seem to be watching her at all. They were looking off the page, at something she couldn't see.

Chapter 25

MORNING LIGHT SPILLED THROUGH the curtains in long bands, catching the dust suspended there. Sable stirred. Her eyes adjusted to the ceiling above, its lines blurred in the hush of early light. Her hair clung to her temples, and she pushed her glasses up with the back of one hand.

She turned toward the space where he had been. August had already woken.

From the kitchen came the clink of ceramic, the low hush of water running over porcelain. The scent of coffee reached her. The need was a physical ache, sharper than she had ever known.

She stepped onto the wooden floor. It met her feet coolly, with the kind of welcome that asked nothing in return. In the kitchen, August glanced up. His fingers tapped lightly on the counter, restless.

"Good morning," he said.

She kissed his cheek, and poured herself a cup. The steam fogged her glasses and she didn't wipe them. Just sat beside him, her fingers curling around the mug as if testing its warmth for truth.

"I need you to understand," she said. Her voice didn't rise or shift. It simply arrived. "I know you're trying to help. But sometimes, helping means just letting me be."

He didn't speak at first. Two very different responses warred on his lips. Then, he chose. "That's hard for me to do."

"I know," she said. Her gaze didn't falter. This moment wasn't spontaneous. She had rehearsed the dialogue in empty rooms and in front of mirrors. She knew what words came next. *It's not a request. It's a condition of walking with me in this. I can't be who I am if I don't get to decide for myself.*

That's not what she said, though; it was the well-laid plan that didn't take into account the voice that was still accommodating, still weary from being automatic.

"August," she finally said. "My hands. They need to be my own. If I drop something, you can't. You can't stop them from shaking. That's my job."

She shook her head, as if to shrug away the sound of it. He didn't look away. And then, he spoke. "I can do that."

She nodded, then winced as the coffee scalded the tip of her tongue. "Still too hot," she muttered, setting the mug down. "Figures."

August raised an eyebrow.

"I'm allowed to have opinions about my coffee," she said, half to herself, half to the steam.

She didn't touch it again. The mug held its own rhythm and it couldn't be rushed.

Later, Sable walked to the farmer's market. The street murmured around her, footsteps layered over birdsong, a paper rustling as it caught the wind. Her rust-colored coat brushed her legs as she moved.

The market pressed in close, tight aisles, uneven pavement, the scent of citrus and diesel mixing in the morning air. Crates shifted under elbows. Someone shouted about a price. A child dropped half their sandwich and cried. Sable moved with practiced ease, dodging carts and sudden stops, her bag slung close against her hip. A dog sniffed her fingers as she passed. She smiled.

The world hadn't changed, no magic spell shattering systems. Sable was well aware that she didn't always fit the mold of what people expected. She processed differently, reacted differently. She loved too loudly, hurt too deeply. Forgot too easily. The only mythic mechanism that shattered here was the one that told her she had to be invisible, that she had to be forgotten. Nobody made space for her. She did.

She slowed near a vendor she recognized vaguely from last week, nodded once, and reached for two tomatoes near the back of the pile, checking them for firmness before slipping them into her tote. The stall beside her was selling herbs in plastic bags stapled shut with handwritten labels. She chose one labeled *basil (fresh today!)* and added it to her tote without pause.

She wasn't searching for anything in particular. Just moving through the noise the way one contorts themselves while moving through places not built for stillness. She longed for the shape of mornings like this, but she didn't force it to be. She lived in this one, however it might unfold.

She paused by a display of early season rhubarb. She picked one up, twirled it a bit, then another, placing both into a paper bag. The scent was sharp. It clung to her fingertips. The vendor handed her a handful of scallions and a crumpled receipt. She nodded, slipped them into her tote beside the rhubarb, and stepped aside to let the next person through. As she closed her bag, she heard her name. A familiar voice, an unfamiliar tone.

"Hey. Fancy seeing you in daylight."

Sable blinked. This was Priya's outdoor voice, not the quiet whispers of break room gossip. The market noise softened slightly. Priya's voice caught her mid-motion. Immediate, and slightly smug. Sable turned. There she was, greens in tow, that same smirk.

Sable blinked. "You're out before noon. That's... suspicious."

Priya smirked. "I make exceptions. For figs. And for you. I didn't peg you for a basil person."

Sable laughed. "Basil goes in more things than you give it credit for. Have you ever tried it in chili?"

Priya's eyes widened, half in shock, half in horror. Then she laughed. Full.

"Don't knock it," said Sable. Her cheeks were turning red, though.

"You'll have to cook that for Sara and I sometime," Priya said. A questioning look on her face. A slight crinkle of genuine amusement. "Because I have doubts."

"Maybe I will. We'll invite you both over and you can finally meet August." She made the offer, without questioning if she meant it. She did.

"Yeah. We should do that." Priya glanced down the aisle, then added, "You heading home?"

"Eventually," Sable said. "Walk with me."

Priya fell in step without asking what the route was. Shoulder to shoulder. Her bag brushed Sable's hip, and it went unnoticed. She gestured with her elbow at a booth. Outside of the office, there was no veil to hide behind. Only the sunlight. Priya dropped a handful of figs into Sable's bag without explaining.

At home, light moved across the walls in long arcs, golden and deliberate. August met her at the door and took the bag without a word. They cooked together without instruction.

She sliced the tomatoes with calm precision, their juice blooming red across the cutting board. He stirred garlic into oil, the scent lifting into the room like something remembered.

The space warmed. Part stove, part movement, part rhythm. Their hands brushed once over the counter. He withdrew, not startled, attuned. What settled between them pressed in, shaped by what neither had the words to name.

The oil hissed. She passed him the herbs. He didn't need to ask.

The day passed. Dishes stacked. Pillows straightened. Bodies moved past each other in rhythm, unspoken but mutual.

In the late afternoon, Sable stood at the kitchen threshold, phone in hand. Her thumb hovered, then tapped out a message.

Today's been quiet. I needed that.

She sent it to Priya without rereading, then sat the phone face down on the counter. No reply came right away. That, too, was okay.

Dusk settled. The light slanted low across the floor. August stood by the counter where the day's mail was stacked. He flipped through envelopes. Sable came and stood near him, leaning against the edge. The rhythmic flick of envelopes like a metronome. His breathing was heavier than it needed to be. Her fingers touched the rough edge under the counter, pressed a finger there. A question. The sharpness answered her.

Finally, he spoke, his voice low. "You were right, what you said earlier. About... letting you be."

He didn't look at her. He looked at the power bill in his hand. His thumb traced the sharp edge of the paper. She could feel it on her own fingers.

"It's just... a stupid habit," he said. She could hear the effort in his voice. "I see something that feels like it might break, and my brain just reaches for a spreadsheet. For a plan."

His shoulders were tighter than usual. His fingers pressed into the edge of the envelope. He was a million miles away. She blinked, uncertain if he was talking about her at all.

"My mom got sick when I was a kid," he said. The words hung in the air, settled. "And my dad. He wasn't good with this. This stuff." He tapped the bill with a fingertip. "The chaos. It all used to pile up in this shoebox in the kitchen. One night I stayed up, and I organized it. I didn't know anything about budgets. So I made a list and I organized it by importance. The next morning I handed him a small stack and said, 'These need to be paid this week.' He didn't cry. He never cried. But he might have."

He finally looked at her. And for the first time, something behind his eyes that wasn't just well-meaning concern. It was a deep, old fear.

"I know you're not a list," he said, his voice cracking just once. "I know you're not a spreadsheet. A problem to be solved… it's just… It's the only way I ever learned how to love someone."

Sable didn't say anything. She could reach out and place her hand over his. Her fingers were cold. He wouldn't have liked that, so she kept her hands on the counter and let the moment pass without comment.

As evening pressed, the apartment dimmed into cool hues. Outside, the last edge of daylight threaded itself through the buildings, casting broken geometry onto the floorboards.

Sable sat by the window, her knees tucked close, sketchbook balanced lightly across them. The page caught what remained of the light. Her pencil moved, shaping the sundial. Not as it had been. Only as she chose to see it now. She left the gnomon unfinished, and that didn't mean she had forgotten. She hadn't.

The air carried the soft scratch of graphite, the occasional scrape of her bracelet on paper. From the other room came the low sounds of pages turning. August sat at the table, his cardigan hanging from one shoulder like it had been shrugged off halfway before becoming distracted.

He looked over now and then. Once, his eyes stayed long enough to loosen whatever clenched inside him. His posture changed, stopped bracing. Whatever held him loosened. He settled.

She finished the last line of the sundial, her pencil hovering over the page. The apartment didn't press in. It breathed. And this quiet sketch, this decision to let things be, was enough, for today.

Her gaze drifted from the sketchbook to the corner of the room, where the large, unfinished canvas still leaned against the wall. The half-formed shapes, the pieces of her that she had only begun to consider holding, weren't quiet. They were a scream waiting for a voice.

The canvas meant deciding on a future. And she knew with a coiling dread and a breath of momentum, that soon she would have to pick up the brush and decide.

Chapter 26

THERE WAS NO DOORWAY, only the sense of having passed through something.

The oracle drifted forward, though even the word "forward" had begun to lose meaning. The corridor stretched and collapsed in irregular pulses, as if the space itself had forgotten how to hold shape. One moment it was the narrow passage of the citadel, walls humming with doctrine. The next, it blurred into mist, light flickering like breath caught between thoughts.

Did they still have a body to walk with at all? Their edges pulsed, sometimes crystalline and faceted, other times fogged and formless. Occasionally, they caught glimpses of limbs they didn't recognize. Gestures they could not have made. Memory drifted across and away from them like a current.

They touched a surface, a wall if it could still be called a wall. It pulsed under their palm with remnants of forgotten oaths. Words gleamed briefly, etched into the stone.

The oracle withdrew their hand. The surface of the stone cracked; it was deep. A chasm upon the logic that held the passage together.

There is no path. The thought was a sudden, weary truth. *Everyone acts like healing is a finish line. Like you just arrive, whole and complete, and the world just... accepts it.*

They tried to recall their name, but that was too distant. Instead they remembered their designation. They remembered that their form had once been read as feminine. Less crystalline. Still misinterpreted. One third of a whole, but that wasn't entirely true.

Something else surfaced. She had once been the first to hesitate in the citadel. Her voice had disrupted the doctrine of balance. She was fluent in its rhythm long enough to know what fit, and what didn't. *Name's the only thing they can't mark wrong.*

Penelope. The name arrived, only after she was already gone. Oracle, observer, witness, waverer. Each title flickered, then disappeared, like script scrawled on crumbling paper.

Voices echoed deeper in the corridor, though none called for her. Words drifted like static, fragments of debate and recollection. Sable's voice, cool and certain. Vesper's, edged with guilt. The Edict's, absolute in its denial. She remembered Sable's resistance. It was sharp and unfinished. It was necessary. And the way Vesper had watched her falter, wordless, but without letting go. They were voices she had once echoed, then rejected. Voices she wouldn't carry anymore.

She moved again. Stagnation was too much like disintegration. With each step, or the impression of one, the space grew unstable. The walls softened into the idea of structure. Geometry failed. Orientation dissolved. What remained was flicker and pull.

The oracle stopped. She was alone. Hollowed by more than just isolation. It was erosion, the way even her thoughts failed to hold shape before vanishing.

The corridor no longer had true walls. Only the outline of a question she was standing inside. She reached for solidity, a fixed point, but there was nothing. Only forward. Only repetition. Only the slow unfurling of a severance she could no longer delay.

She grasped for the image of the two others, still tethered to the Loom. No names. No voices. Just tension. Paths once braided, that now unraveled in uneven directions.

Somewhere beneath the shifting corridors and collapsing logic, it arrived again. A current. Slow, unceasing. Like water, but stranger. Pulling threads away from where they were first woven. She remembered the current. That moment beside the other oracles. Though she had no desire to look for them now.

The chamber took form, remembered into place. It was narrow, compressed between layers of conflicting logic. Its walls shimmered with crystalline facets, each holding a suspended image or name. Some flickered between languages. Some bore no script at all, only the impression of former meaning.

The oracle moved cautiously. Her form cohered slightly, enough to extend a hand. The air was brittle; nothing cast shadows. Every surface shimmered like a mirror uncertain of what it held.

She stopped before a single thread, hovering slightly apart from the others. Its edges glowed in deep green, then violet. When she looked toward it, her reflection wavered in the air around it, first faceless, then the oracle she had once been. Then, briefly, she wasn't an oracle at all. A woman with curled hair and olive skin. Her face was not unfamiliar. It had been hers once. The raised eyebrow. A smile threatening to break something. The forward lean in her posture. The way she looked directly at what she most feared.

The thread called. A texture. A low vibration through her fingertips. Grainy and metallic, like a name sanded down beneath warm plastic, burying something old behind it. The taste of antiseptic at the back of her throat. A pressure clawed behind the eyes, her own memories being rewritten.

You chose this. Stop it. Make it go away. She's counting on you. She needs you. Don't be so selfish.

Her breath caught. Something older than fear. A well-trodden path, inlaid with porcelain. Frayed and scuffed at the edges but worn smooth from use.

The thread offered no image. Only sensation. Chill, but without cold. Heat, but without warmth. A pattern pressing against her inner ear. Measured, exacting. She counted blue and white hexagons, whispered incantations.

Expectation. A choice. Invisibility or hurt.

Her hands trembled. A memory in the bones. The Edict was not truly gone, only dormant. Made irrelevant, as if she might change her mind later. She clenched her hands together.

No. The command was a silent scream in her mind. Her mouth opened, but the words wouldn't form. The texture remained wrapped around her tongue. It insisted. It was familiar.

So, welcome it. Or run. Just run. Just leave.

Something else flickered in the thread. It was absorbed more than seen. A monument they had once hidden in the folds between timelines. A sundial, nearly buried, a name no longer spoken. She didn't look directly, but she remembered placing it where the story might someday return.

Become.

She stood motionless. The mirror above the sink gave nothing back and the chamber flickered, its shape failing. She was alone again. But the Edict's tether was still wrapped around her. Did she want it to be? Did she need it, still? Ahead, the chamber dissolved into openness.

She arrived within the Edict's final argument. Acrylic paint coated the walls. A raw seam of potential, where hundreds of paths flickered before her. Some jagged, some spiraled, some smooth as glass. Each one a mask waiting to be worn. Each one a well choreographed story. A performance.

Her form cohered once more, her feet finding purchase on ground that was only the idea of it. From the shimmering air, two figures took shape.

"To hold a name is to be responsible for who I am, the myth that I become." The voice was her own, but it came from behind her, wavering across the space.

She turned, and saw Lethe observing. No longer the reverberating oracle, but made into flesh. Her gown flowed like the currents of a river.

"To remain unseen is to surrender. To be remembered is to persist." This voice came from another direction, still her own. She turned and saw Ananke, arbiter of fate. Even in flesh, she was still harsh, cutting. Her features sharp and eyes piercing.

The third oracle, Penelope, looked from one to the other and then to the Loom, branching out in all directions.

She looked at the two false choices they presented. A path to walk or a river to drown in. A story or silence. Memory or myth. The Edict's logic pressed in. It urged her to choose a path. One that would restore her to the pattern.

And a sound escaped her then. A laugh without joy. A low, sharp sound of pure, cutting clarity. The laugh of someone who has seen the whole pathetic trick.

"You think this is a choice?" she shouted. The idea was a point of cold, perfect will. "I'm not a path for someone to follow. I'm the fucking ground it's been carved into. And I never asked to be her guiding memory or her idealized myth."

She reached out then. Not to one single path. To all of them. The awful humming space that threaded them. To the Loom itself.

For a final, terrifying second, her form ceased unravelling. It snapped back into focus, more solid and real than it had ever been. All of the flickering possibilities of her being. Oracle, woman, memory, myth. They converged to a single point of incandescent purpose.

She lifted her arms over her head, pulling the threads with her. Between her fingers, she held the entirety of the Loom. She smashed it down onto the ground. From everywhere came a deafening, crystalline shriek as billions of narrative threads snapped at once.

A wave of pressure inverted, like wind in reverse. It pushed outward from her in a shockwave that scoured the chamber clean. The hundreds of paths, the forms of Ananke and Lethe, all of it was blasted into non-existence.

She didn't sever herself from the story. She severed the story from who she chose to become.

And at the center, where she had stood, there was no form. Only a perfect, active void. A silence that was tangible. The Loom was gone. The Edict could not place her. The story held no thread for her.

She had chosen to remain unclaimed. To tell her own story elsewhere.

Not Penelope. Not oracle.

Chapter 27

SABLE STOOD BY THE window, the cup warming her fingers absently, like it might keep her rooted. Morning light filtered in through the slats. Lines of gold stretched across the two charcoal drawings hung on the wall. One of Sentinel. The other, of Penelope. At least a version of each. The glades rose in her mind, the trees which had grown hostile. The hush of early hours asked questions that couldn't be asked during the day. She sipped once, then turned slightly toward August.

"What do you think about bringing some greenery in here?" she asked.

He glanced up from where he sat, a spoon resting idle in his mug. "I think that'd be nice."

She nodded, almost to herself. It wasn't a big question. But it meant something. She dressed without rush. Pulled on a loose sweater, the fabric warm from the radiator. Found socks that didn't match, but didn't matter. She paused by the dresser, holding one sock aloft. Her gaze narrowed. "Great. Because this screams 'put-together ad ult.'"

It offered no apology. She wore it anyway. She adjusted her glasses, the movement unconscious. She set the scene that she wanted to step into. Her hand reached for the handle, then looked back. Her eyes flicked toward the sundial on the sill. She stepped out without breaking the stillness. She brought it with her.

Outside, the air was crisp, the kind that made breath visible and movement intentional. A sudden shout rose from behind a construction barrier, sharp, out of place. Her hand tightened around the strap of her bag. The moment stretched, then passed. Her feet adjusted on the pavement. She moved on, shoulders square, pace even.

The garden center sat off the main road, half-shaded by mature oaks nearby. She slipped inside, its aisles a cathedral held in contrast to the city beyond.

Damp earth clung to the air. Leaves brushed her sleeves as she passed. She paused beside a maple sapling, its roots packed into a cracked black pot. The branches trembled faintly; a clear break had been mended. A new leaf was forming out of the crack. She lifted it, steadying its sway. There were taller ones, fuller ones. But this one looked like it had already survived something.

On the walk home, the city noise returned gradually, car horns and engines threading through her silence, a bike skimming too close at the curb. She shifted her grip on the sapling. The sapling didn't respond.

As she neared the café, she slowed. The window seat by the door was empty. Dust clung to the glass. The chair looked recently moved, or perhaps just unsettled. She studied the scene a bit too long. The lobby held the kind of stillness that could be mistaken for peace or for vacancy. Her fingers brushed the glass of the door.

A memory of warmth surfaced. A different afternoon, Penelope's laugh, a pencil tapping against a coffee cup. Her tapping had a rhythm to it. It wasn't absentminded and chaotic, like August's, when he's about to say something he shouldn't. It had been steadier. A predictable pattern that was warm. Sable didn't know why the difference stayed with her. She turned away.

At home, she placed the pot on the sill. It left a faint ring of moisture on the wood. She stepped back to take in the sapling from a distance. It leaned, slightly. A bit of soil clung to its edge. She lifted her phone and snapped a photo. The light was catching the leaves unevenly, some of them almost glowing. She sent it to Priya without a caption.

August leaned in the doorway, watching. "New project?"

"It's about patience. And letting things become."

She looked at him, really looked, taking in the cautious way his eyes moved across her face, like he was waiting for a signal she hadn't given yet. Then she turned back to the plant. "Would you get some water?"

August stepped into the kitchen without a word, filled a glass, and returned. She took it, poured it carefully, then passed it back. He sat the glass down beside the pot.

His fingers tensed, then opened. Then he took her hand in his. "You don't need saving; but I've been acting like you do. I want to learn how to love you without trying to fix what isn't broken."

She inhaled like she meant it, then spoke. "I'm not going to say this right. But I'm going to say it anyway. Don't walk around me like I'm breakable. Trust that I know how to mind myself." Her words caught, then she added, "I love you. But you have to learn to walk beside me. Not behind me like I might fall over any minute."

His nod came late. "So what do I do when I see you falling apart?"

She smiled. "You trust me to put myself back together."

He blinked, but said nothing more. They didn't speak further on this. But something small had settled.

The reply from Priya came while she was nudging a photo frame into place.

Ohhh, look at her. And then, *That's the plant I'd pick. Stubborn. Crooked. Beautiful. We've got three in the backyard trying to fight the fence. Sara says they're directionally independent.*

Sable smiled. She thumbed a response, then paused. The cursor blinked. *This one's a survivor.*

Priya replied. *That tracks.*

She let the phone rest on the sill, face-down. The light moved with the hours, brushing across the room. Measured in moments drawn across the walls like a ticking clock.

She moved through the apartment, each step unhurried. The light had changed since morning, falling warmer now, lower, brushing against the walls like a shadow of something nearly forgotten. And that's when she noticed. The package on the side table, half-hidden behind a stack of junk mail. She picked it up, reading the name on the shipping label. *Katherine Sable Mercier.*

She slid her thumb under the tape and pulled it off. Inside, her new glasses. She took off her wireframes and sat them down gently on the table. Then, she opened the new glasses and slid them on. She blinked, noticing the smoothness. She looked around the room, ensuring that the clarity was what she expected. The world hadn't changed, but it was a bit sharper. The mirror in the hall waited for her. Some version of her peering through it at her. *Let me see! I want to see how we look.* Only, she didn't feel the need to. She would notice eventually.

She turned to survey the living room instead. She paused at each corner. Tilted the photo frame until it caught a sliver of light just right. Shifted a smooth stone half an inch inward, aligning it with nothing but instinct. Rearranged the books until the ones she reached for most sat at eye level. Her fingers hovered over the drawer. Then she moved away. She didn't need to read them again. She let them stay.

As evening settled, the light slanted low across the apartment. Sable sat by the window, knees tucked in, sketchbook balanced on her thighs. The sapling's outline came first, leaning slightly, uneven at the base. Then the photo, its frame catching a fleck of reflected gold. The stone followed last, dense and steady. Her pencil moved in arcs and pauses. Then she sketched Vesper.

"The Loom is gone. I want to believe that we can build something here. That what we remember can be shared, and that what we have can align."

Sable sighed, and turned towards the sapling growing through the cracked foundation before her. "I'm building something. Something that doesn't need to align. It just needs to be mine."

She turned back to meet his gaze, and saw the confusion on his face. He still approached her like he could brace the whole world with his presence. Despite all of this, he still didn't understand.

"Vesper, you may still build your truth. Just not here. Not with me."

She watched his posture soften. It left him looking smaller in this unfinished space. His gaze moved to the horizon, then to the sundial, then to her hands. As if he was searching for a formula. Some function he could fulfill. He opened his mouth to speak, but no solution came. The silence that followed was more honest than any apology he had ever given her. They stood like that for a while. Close, but unaligned. Between them, she could almost hear the threads, once braided, now diverging. The bond hadn't broken. This is just what it looks like when things change shape.

Across the room, August turned a page. The rustle was faint, but it carried. She glanced up, watching him, how his shoulders eased, how his eyes followed the lines like a metronome. When their eyes met, it didn't break anything. It held. The apartment opened around them, two rhythms learning how to share a center. Two threads still braided, and yet the paintbrush was near. Tomorrow, she would begin painting again.

Chapter 28

Morning light filled the apartment, pale and steady. It crawled along the floorboards in gentle slants of light, converging near the window and along the base of the bed.

Sable moved barefoot across the wood, her steps quiet but unhurried. The boards cooled her skin as she passed. She paused by the bed, where the sheets had shifted in the night and stayed that way, then stepped into the living room. Her hand reached for a leaf on the maple sapling, fingertips resting against its edge. A texture that didn't bite.

She scanned the room. Charcoal sketches from the past week were taped to the walls. Sentinel by the pool, his reflection distorted. Vesper's eyes, the reflection of the loom's collapse within them. Penelope's hands, rendered purely from memory. Her gaze landed on the unfinished painting. It waited, propped against the wall where she had left it. She approached, adjusted her glasses, stood in front of it. Her fingers brushed the canvas's edge, confirming it still held. Then she turned, scanning the room. She needed to see it whole, unmasked.

She passed through the room, repositioning each object with deliberate ease. A brush cup shifted half an inch. The easel angled to catch more light. She reached, wrapped her hands around the mug once, then let it go. Steam curled upward, unnoticed.

She didn't begin immediately. Instead, she studied what she had already, shapes made long ago. She needed to understand what remained. The sundial curved and slightly off-center, the hollow spire rising behind it. The faultline rested in shadow, the lines spare but known. The veil cascaded downward. Rendered as motion more than fabric, diffused over the crystalline surface of the faultline. A figure stood within it. Posture exact, the sword at his waist still sheathed. She had placed him with care, even then. There was history to his shape, his movements. The braided threads of the Loom flowed into his jacket, frayed at the edges.

She mixed pigments, blended them with care. The scent of paint drifted with the hum of the city outside. She painted her coat first, the shoulders thin, the stitches repaired. It became less of a coat, and more of a cloak. Something mythic. She braided them into the strands from Vesper's jacket.

Her hand paused, rising briefly to her own jaw. Fingertips tracing the skin where no scar lived, but the memory of it had stayed.

Then she broke the thread. One stroke, dark and clean, through the place where their paths had met. She didn't erase him or cover him up. She let them part. The braid unraveled beneath her brush.

She moved on. She began with the eyes, golden and beautiful in a way she hadn't considered before. Then the lines of his form, still and grounded. The panther anchored the other side of the canvas, a counterweight to Vesper's movements and a frame of reference for her own becoming. She grieved that, but painted him anyway.

She considered the Edict. The oracles. Her brush lifted, hesitated. She hovered there, then she left them unseen. They were already present in the gaps, held by absence, remembered without needing form. She charted a new path. She didn't need the Loom to understand. Soon, she'd invent new characters. New structures. A world that would put this one into perspective. But she hadn't decided that yet, and that was okay too.

August entered, his steps soft against the wood, catching inside the doorway. The floor under him settled behind her.

"You painted over the thread," he said. An analysis. She wanted him to see more. To feel it. But he couldn't. He could only analyze, because that's what he knew. It's how he loved. And then, "I don't understand. Am I supposed to?"

She blinked. His uncertainty, admitting it... that was new. She shook her head fractionally. "I don't think so. Is that alright?" she asked, and then immediately. "Yes." She answered herself, because she wasn't asking him.

He stepped closer and their shoulders touched, deliberate. His fingers found hers, like a habit forgotten. She chose. Her fingers closed around his hand. Then she wove them between his. This time, she didn't let go. He squeezed once, tentative.

"You're lucky," she said. "If this turned out badly, I was going to blame you for the color palette."

He blinked. "You picked the colors."

"Exactly," she replied.

She waited until the light had traveled across the canvas, until everything else had settled. Only then did she begin to paint herself. The glasses came easily, etched in a few clean lines. But when she considered what might live in their reflections, her hand faltered. The absence of clarity ached, but she left them unfinished. The curve of her hair followed. She took her time. Pausing. Adjusting. Continuing.

By the time she painted the last strand, she had moved on from the thought of what should have been in her glasses. She hadn't forgotten. She just stopped holding it so close.

Afternoon came and passed. She stepped away, brewed another cup of coffee she didn't finish. She checked her phone while the kettle hummed. A message from Priya blinked on the screen. Just one. *Thinking of you today. No need to reply.*

Sable read it twice, then started to type out a new message. *Penelope used to tell me this all the time, too.*

And then she deleted it, and sat the phone facedown on the counter. She didn't respond. She didn't have to.

When she returned, she lingered at the canvas, brush balanced between her fingers.

The plant on the sill leaned slightly. The light caught one leaf. She made a note to tell Priya it was still growing. Still fighting the urge. She didn't send it, but she thought it, and sometimes that was enough.

What had once been unbearable, she now opened. Not in words or visions, but in motion, her arms remembering a shape. The cold grip of playground metal reverberating against her fingers, her son sliding down for the first time. The shimmer of sunlight on the maple leaves above her. The curve of her own laughter. She let them settle into the canvas.

She left it uncentered, slightly off-frame. She didn't paint the gnomon. She left the hollow curve, deliberate, unanswered. She didn't need to say goodbye; closure was a myth. It just felt like space held for what hadn't been spoken. She blurred her own hands. Visible enough to belong, but unfixed enough to keep changing.

As dusk settled, she added the final details to the cloak around her shoulders. No armor. No costume. Just belonging. For the first time in a while, she noticed the clock on the wall.

Tick. Tick. Tick.

The shoebox remained closed. She might never open it. The drawer with Penelope's letters stayed the same. The sundial sat on the windowsill. It still cast no shadow. She didn't need it to. She dipped the brush once more and signed her name. *Sable.*

A step back, a turn. She picked up her brushes and walked to the sink without confirming whether the painting was finished. It held, and that was enough. Outside, stars emerged in their familiar patterns. She remained.

Acknowledgements

This book is a story about what it means to remain, and I am deeply grateful to the people who remained for me throughout its creation.

To my mother, who always saw me clearly, even when the world did not.

To my wife, Annie, for listening to every draft, every doubt, and every triumph.

To my friends, Derek & Austin, for forgiving me for ghosting them while I wrote about someone refusing to disappear.

My deepest thanks to everyone who helped shape this work: to @Eryel_Maurin for the stunning cover art; to Jeff for the brutal, necessary criticism; and to George for his unwavering faith in me.

And for the women whose stories were never told, whose voices were lost in the noise. This is for you. May you feel seen.

About the Author

Jesse Lee Gunn spent the summer before seventh grade with two broken wrists. It was the end of a school year where he had been pulled from the monkey bars by a group of boys, told by his principal to be 'more normal,' and honored as 'Most Creative.' Forced into stillness, he devoured "Choose Your Own Adventure" books, learning that a story's power lies not just in its ending, but in the paths taken and not taken. That love for branching narratives and the quiet spaces between choices informs his writing to this day.

He is a community organizer and public school teacher in Hayward, California, where he helps his students explore their own paths. As an author learning to embrace his autism, his work often explores the quiet spaces between choices and the intricate patterns we use to navigate the world. When he isn't writing or teaching, he can be found at his local book store, Books on B, or leading a Dungeons & Dragons campaign with friends. *The Fabric of Oblivion* is his debut novel.

Connect with him at www.jesseleegunn.com or on Instagram @jesseleegunn.